W9-AQL-680

06/2018

ROUGH JUSTICE

A CAINSVILLE NOVELLA

KELLEY ARMSTRONG

Illustrations by Xavière Daumarie

SUBTERRANEAN PRESS 2018

First Edition

ISBN
978-1-59606-856-8

Subterranean Press
PO Box 190106
Burton, MI 48519

subterraneanpress.com

ONE

OLIVIA

TONIGHT I would watch a man die for his crimes. I would hunt him down and let a pack of giant black hounds rip him to death and send his soul to the afterlife, and I would trust that he had done something to deserve it.

I was struggling with that concept.

Not the part where I'd hunt him or even watch him die. I'd seen a man torn apart by a cŵn before, and while I didn't intend to closely observe the process, I did not have an issue with the overall idea of it. Otherwise, I wouldn't be here.

I believed in the Cŵn Annwn, in their purpose on earth. The Welsh Wild Hunt, tasked with wreaking vengeance on humans who murder those with fae blood. Did those crimes deserve such a fate? Sometimes. Other times, though, it was indeed rough justice. But justice it was. When you take a life—intentionally and maliciously—you must accept that you may receive the same in return.

My problem with tonight's Hunt? The part where I didn't know what our quarry had actually done.

I had chosen not to know. I'd seen that as purpose. Resolution. Faith, too, which doesn't come easily to me. I trusted that the Cŵn Annwn were justified in their actions, and so for my first Hunt, I would prove that by not asking for details.

Yeah…

A noble sentiment, which lasted only until the moment of truth loomed.

I sat on my horse, leaning forward, hand rubbing her neck, trying to calm my nerves with her warmth. She felt those nerves, though, and her left ear twitched.

"Dwi'n iawn, Rhyddhad," I said, reassuring her I was okay.

A soft whinny suggested I might be lying.

Rhyddhad looked like a regular horse—a young gray mare— just as the cŵns looked like regular hounds. They were, in their way. That is, they weren't shape-shifting humanoid fae. But they were fae beasts, and they understood us better than mortal ones.

Rhyddhad and I were on an empty stretch of country road, outside Chicago. Waiting for our quarry to arrive.

The Hunt must take place in a forest. That was traditionally the domain of the Cŵn Annwn, and back in ancient Wales, the restriction had been no restriction at all as people passed through forest regularly. It was trickier in the modern world. And in Chicago? A city of three million people…? Let's just say that it was a good thing the local Cŵn Annwn pack had been here for centuries, with time to adjust and improvise. Time to learn how to get even the most urban-dwelling killer to a patch of woods.

It helped, too, that they only needed to conduct a proper Hunt a few times a year. That meant plenty of time to use their tricks—both human and supernatural—to get their prey where they wanted him.

This time, they were lucky—their target worked in Chicago but lived outside it. He passed daily along this wooded road, and he often drove past dark.

It'd been almost a week ago when Ioan—leader of the local Cŵn Annwn—came to me and said, "We have one. Are you ready?"

I was. There wasn't any doubt of that. I was the new Mallt-y-Nos. Matilda of the Night. Matilda of the Hunt. I had accepted that role, and along with it, I accepted this responsibility.

When headlights bobbed down the empty road, hooves tapped across the pavement, a rider coming to my side, a cŵn loping beside him, her tongue lolling.

"Looks like we have a winner," Ricky said as he reined in. "Dark sedan headed this way, right on time."

He smiled, but it wasn't his usual grin. He was on edge, too, and his horse—Tywysog Du—shook his head, breath streaming in the cool spring air.

"We doing this?" he said.

"I guess so."

He inched Tywysog Du closer and reached to squeeze my arm. Ricky Gallagher. Former lover, current best friend—a feat I was still amazed we'd managed. It took work, but it was important to both of us, and six months later, we were settled into the new relationship.

This would be Ricky's first Hunt, too. The first time we fully inhabited our ancient roles—me as Matilda and him as Arawn, Lord of the Otherworld, legendary king of the Cŵn Annwn. There was a third party in this configuration. Gwynn ap Nudd, even more legendary king of the fae, the Tylwyth Teg. But Gabriel had no place here. Not tonight.

"Is that the car?" Ioan asked, his quiet voice traveling through the silence.

Another of the Cŵn Annwn—Meic—peered down the road with binoculars. Yes, just regular binoculars. The Huntsmen were blessed with near-perfect night vision, but not bionic sight, and unlike most fae, they embraced human tech.

"It's definitely a dark sedan," Meic said. "Could be an Audi..."

"You realize you have an expert, right?" Ricky called to him.

Ioan chuckled and waved for Meic to bring the binoculars to me.

My Cŵn Annwn blood gave me decent night vision, but it wasn't like theirs, and I had to squint to make out the oncoming vehicle.

"We've got a BMW," I said, as it came over a dip a hundred feet away.

I only needed to nudge Rhyddhad. She knew what that meant: get the hell away from the roadside before some poor stranger goes into a tailspin seeing a pack of giant hounds and horsemen.

Human folklore said that if you spotted the Hunt, you'd die. That wasn't exactly true. Yes, if you spotted them, and they were there *for* you, I'd suggest an emergency call to check your life insurance policy. But for any culture with Wild Hunt folklore, the fear of them was ingrained, and the Cŵn Annwn preferred not to send innocent humans into mindless panic, especially when they were behind the wheel of a motor vehicle.

So the horses and hounds headed into the field, not unlike city kids playing road hockey when someone called "Car!"

I watched the vehicle as it passed and... "Shit!"

There was the dark blue Audi we were waiting for—a few car lengths behind the BMW.

"Brenin!" Ioan shouted, alerting the alpha cŵn.

The hound whipped around, but he was too far from the road. The closest to it was Ricky's cŵn, Lloergan. She suffered from old injuries, meaning she hadn't kept up when we bolted for the field.

"Lloe?" Ricky called, but she was already veering as Brenin barked a command.

Lloergan ran back to the road. The BMW was gone, the Audi coming fast. The cŵn wasn't going to make it. And if she *did*...

Lloergan leapt onto the road right in front of the Audi. I shouted, "No!" as the car went into a spin.

"I can't see Lloe," I whispered, leaning over Rhyddhad's neck. "Where's...?"

I spotted her then...lying on the road.

Ricky started forward, but Ioan cut him off, saying, "No."

Ricky let out a growl, and his horse stamped.

"She's getting up," I said as I peered through the binoculars. "She's limping, though."

Ricky cursed under his breath. Tywysog Du continued stamping.

"Wait," Ioan said. "Just wait."

The Audi had stopped spinning. The BMW driver either didn't notice what happened behind him or pretended he didn't, as the car's rear lights faded into the night.

The Audi driver's door opened. A man stepped out. As soon as he saw Lloergan, she toppled over.

The man looked around, as if assessing his chances of getting back into his vehicle and taking off. Not exactly a choice that warranted the death penalty, but if I was looking for signs that this guy was an asshole, I could take this.

He gave Lloergan only a cursory glance. Then he bent to examine the front end of his car.

Yep, definitely an asshole.

The man got down on all fours to check for damage on the undercarriage.

"The front end's fine," Ricky murmured.

I was about to ask what he meant when Lloergan pushed up, slowly. The guy didn't notice—she was behind him, and he was intent on seeing what damage she'd done to his precious car.

Through the binoculars, I saw her lips pull back in a growl. The man glanced over his shoulder and then gave a very satisfying start.

Lloergan advanced, her head lowered, fur on end, inflating the big dog to the size of a bear. The guy scrambled up. She let out a snarl loud enough for me to hear.

The guy inched toward his open driver's door. He made it three steps. Then Brenin came tearing across the field, two other cŵns on his heels. The man bolted for his car, but Brenin was racing across the road, and the guy clambered onto the hood of his car instead. He stood up there, looking down at Brenin and Lloergan, the other two dogs approaching. Then he peered along the empty road.

He took out his cell phone. Hit a button. Peered at it.

"Yeah, that's not going to work," Ricky said.

In today's world, if you were beset by giant hounds, help was only a call away. Unless there was a high-tech cell-phone blocker… attached to the collar of the lead hound.

The cŵns circled the car patiently, allowing the man to realize that calling for help wasn't an option. Then Brenin leapt onto the hood. The man slid down into the opening they'd left, and he started to run as the hounds herded him toward the waiting forest.

"And that's our cue," Ioan said, handing Ricky and me each a bundle. "We let the hounds tire him while we dress."

"Our cloaking devices," Ricky said, shaking his out. "Appropriately in the form of an actual cloak."

Ioan waved for one of the others to accompany Ricky into a patch of forest so he could put on his cloak, turning him into a true Huntsman. While Ricky and I had ridden with the Cŵn Annwn on recreational hunts, this would be our first time donning the official costume.

When I started after Ricky, Ioan said, "Wait," and motioned for me to follow him to a larger patch of trees.

As we rode, he said, "Have you changed your mind? About wanting to know what our quarry has done?"

I shook my head, but not before I hesitated a moment too long.

"You can ask what he's done, Liv," he said.

When I didn't respond, he said, "If you think you need to prove anything by not asking, please remember that you aren't the only one who is anxious to do this right. You are our Matilda. The only one we've ever had, and the only one we'll ever get. Having you ride strengthens us. That's why you're doing it, and we realize that, so we want you to be comfortable."

"You know he's guilty."

He nodded, but I meant it as a statement. Huntsmen had the innate ability to see guilt. It was like the old saying about guilt being written on a face. They knew their target deserved their justice, and so they didn't dig deeper. With my Cŵn Annwn blood, I should have that same faith.

"It doesn't work like that," he said.

I gave him a hard look.

He threw up his free hand, the other loosely holding the reins. "If you don't want me to read your thoughts, don't make them so easy to read. It's like speaking and expecting me to not listen. You cannot have our faith because you are not us. Yours would be blind faith. Ours isn't—we know they are guilty. Lacking that ability, you need evidence to develop honest—and open-eyed—faith in our powers. Which is why I urged you to investigate first. That's what you do. It's how your mind works, Liv."

He was right. I was an investigator by trade now, for Gabriel's law firm. But that was the problem. Gabriel was a defense lawyer, so my job was to keep people from what was, sometimes, proper justice. Which I supposed made me a lousy Matilda. But while my father had Cŵn Annwn blood, my mother—like Gabriel—was part fae, and their sense of ethics was a whole lot looser. Put those two sides together, and you got me: someone who was fine with setting a criminal free if the prosecutor failed to do his job, but who also believed that if you committed a crime, you needed to be prepared to pay the price.

"How much do you know about what he did?" I asked.

"His name and the very basics of the crime." He stopped his horse. "If you have any concerns, Ricky can join us on this Hunt, and you'll come the next time after you've done your research and are convinced *that* target is guilty."

"I can't ever know that, short of an actual confession. All the investigation in the world only builds certainty. It never seals it." I shook my head. "No, this is better. You know the guy is guilty, and that's enough. But I will take what you have on him."

"Will that help?"

He told me what he knew. And I immediately saw a problem. A big one.

TWO

GABRIEL

WHILE OLIVIA was off on her first Hunt, Gabriel sat in a bar, drinking with a young woman who very clearly was hoping for more than pleasant conversation. Personally, he'd rather be at home working. Or with Olivia. But that was not permitted, so instead, he was doing her a favor by taking another woman for drinks.

The woman in question was a relatively new assistant state's attorney. So new that she actually thought asking Gabriel to drinks to "discuss their case" was a good idea. It was a common error, though not one that was commonly repeated. Some of the younger attorneys looked at Gabriel, saw a young and unattached attorney and thought they knew exactly how to beat him in court. Oddly, the fact that he hadn't been unattached for the past six months seemed to have no effect on the invitations.

Before Olivia, he had been known to accept invitations, finding them very useful. Not for sex, of course, but for the same reason these lawyers asked him—to gain valuable information. He just happened to be much better at the game than they were.

Gabriel had agreed to tonight's invitation as a gift for Olivia. Something to cheer her up after the Hunt. To distract her, if she needed distracting. Of course he had other ways of distracting her in the short term, but beyond that, she would require more. His gift would be information on a case that was stymieing her, a case to be argued by Amy Keating, the attorney sitting across from him.

Ms. Keating was not particularly enjoying her evening. Gabriel could tell by the way she kept shifting in her seat. And the way she kept ordering refills, growing increasingly frustrated. Gabriel seemed oblivious to her flirting, and *he* wasn't getting refills, which meant she couldn't hope for an alcohol-loosened tongue. In fact, he barely seemed to have touched his drink. He hadn't, actually, not beyond a lip-wetting sip. Gabriel didn't drink unless he was with Olivia and comfortable with letting down his guard. Having an alcoholic drug addict for a mother tended to squelch any interest in social imbibing.

For all Ms. Keating's frustration, though, it was proving to be quite a productive meeting for him. The younger lawyer wasn't very good at this sort of manipulation. Getting information from a source required a degree of quid pro quo. You needed to give something first. The trick was to only provide details they could easily find themselves. Instead, Ms. Keating was luring him in with genuine tidbits, and when she didn't receive nibbles, she threw out bigger lures. The alcohol certainly didn't help her judgment.

What Gabriel really wanted was her cell phone. Ms. Keating was trying to cajole a reluctant witness onto the stand, and Olivia needed his name. Gabriel knew exactly where to find it—in Ms. Keating's call records. While it was possible to obtain those in other ways, this was the safest method. Safe for Gabriel, at least, who'd been picking pockets since he was a child.

When he finally did take the phone from Ms. Keating's open purse, the timing was not so much about the perfect opportunity to steal it, but rather the perfect time to *have* stolen it...as she began glancing about for the ladies room.

When she returned he watched for any sign that she'd realized her phone was missing. If so, he'd slip it onto the floor. But she only sat down and started talking again, and he deftly returned it to her purse. Then, goal accomplished, he had to suppress the urge to leave. That would look suspicious. So they talked, a tedious conversation he could barely bring himself to follow. When his phone dinged with a text, he took it quickly with an "Excuse me."

As he opened the message, Ms. Keating said, "Girlfriend checking up on you?"

"No, she's out for the evening." He caught her look and added, "With Ricky Gallagher."

Ms. Keating's blink confirmed she knew who Ricky was. He hardly needed to divulge that, but he couldn't resist really. Not after she'd smirked when he said Olivia was away, as if Gabriel had snuck out to have drinks with her while Olivia was otherwise occupied.

"Isn't he...the biker?"

Gabriel fixed her with a baleful look. "Mr. Gallagher is the member of a motorcycle club."

"Right, but I mean, weren't they...together?"

"Yes, and now they are friends. Olivia said hello, by the way. I asked her to join us, but her plans with Ricky were apparently more enticing."

Ms. Keating's mouth opened, and nothing came out, which gave him time to read his text. It was from his aunt, which explained why he'd been in no hurry to read it. There was only one reason Rose texted him at this hour, and as he read the message, his stomach tightened.

"I need to go," he said, rising. "A sick relative requires my attention."

She snorted a laugh. "I think you can do better than that, counselor."

He met her gaze, his pale blue eyes fixing on hers, and she shrank back.

"My mother is ill," he said slowly. "I do not appreciate levity."

"I...I'm—"

"If you wish to discuss this case again, please contact Olivia. I suspect you'll find her far more pleasant company. Just do not expect *her* to divulge any useful information on the case, either. Now, good evening, Ms. Keating."

THREE

OLIVIA

I DIDN'T share my misgivings with Ioan. I couldn't, not after I'd said that it was enough for him to know this man—Keith Barent Johnson—was guilty.

It wasn't enough.

I retreated to put on my cloak and focused on that, as if it would help.

A cloak for Matilda.

It was old. Maybe even ancient. Not hers, though. Not the original Matilda's. That wasn't possible. But there had been other iterations of her, like me, through the centuries, and some had taken their place with the Cŵn Annwn. This cloak had belonged to one of those. To a woman whose name I didn't even know, who once stood in a grove like this and donned the cloak for her first ride.

She had chosen the Cŵn Annwn. That was what all Matildas were supposed to do. Choose a side. Cŵn Annwn or Tylwyth Teg. Whichever she chose received the gift of her power, which was even more critical in the modern world, as fae struggled to find the pure elements—clean water, air and earth—that would sustain them.

I hadn't picked a side. I refused to. I looked back at the original story where Matilda died because Gwynn and Arawn needed her to choose between them, between their worlds. Ever since that, the fae and the Huntsmen have been trying to make her choose. But in the beginning, there was just a girl who loved two boys, a girl who was half Cŵn Annwn and half Tylwyth Teg, her best friends the princes of each side. She'd divided her time between the two kingdoms, and the three of them had been inseparable. Best friends, until she'd realized she loved Gwynn as more than a friend, and Arawn couldn't accept that.

When Matilda had been forced to choose, that was when it all went wrong. I decided on her original choice—to divide her time between the two, honor both sides of her self.

It wasn't a perfect solution. In giving part of my power to each, I deprived both of my full strength. But this worked for me. It worked for *us*—Gabriel and Ricky and me.

The Matilda who wore this cloak did choose, though. Did she turn down the Tylwyth Teg...or were they never part of the equation? Did she have an Arawn? Were they friends? Lovers? And Gwynn? Did he lose, or was he, too, never an option, never someone she met? I had seen all configurations, and I knew I was rare—a Matilda who met both her Gwynn and her Arawn, who knew both Tylwyth Teg and Cŵn Annwn. A Matilda who faced all the complications that came with that.

I fingered the cloak. It was dark green wool, lined with silk and trimmed in white fur, with a jeweled clasp. Thick and heavy, it smelled of wood fire and forest.

I slipped it on and...

Horses. I heard horses—the pound of hooves, a snort, a whinny. The smell of pine and moss. A flash of fire, the sizzle and pop. A hound baying. The croak of a raven. Laughter. A wordless voice at my ear. Then a scream, cut short—

"Olivia?"

I snapped out of it and stepped into the open to find Ioan waiting. The other Huntsmen were a few dozen feet away, horses stamping.

It might seem as if we should have been in hot pursuit, but the Huntsmen would let the hounds get Johnson deep into the forest, herding him rather than driving him.

While I'd been talking to Ioan, the other Huntsmen had moved the car to the side of the road, shut the door and turned off the lights and ignition. Johnson would vanish here, leaving only an abandoned vehicle. That was one reason for making sure the hounds got him as far into the woods as possible.

"I'm coming up behind you," a voice said. "Just letting you know it's me."

I could tell it was Ricky by his words, but his voice was distorted, as if booming from deep within the cloak's hood.

"Yep, I got the Darth Vader upgrade, too," Ricky said and took a few deep breaths.

He made light to lift the mood but also to reassure me that he was still Ricky. It didn't sound like him. And it sure as hell didn't look like him.

A dark green cloak enveloped his body from the waist up. Black jodhpurs encased his legs, ending in gleaming riding boots. The hood swallowed his face, and when he turned my way, I caught the red glow of eyes.

"Still me," he said. "However freaky the outfit."

His horse had changed, too, losing its glamour and reclaiming its true form—a massive black stallion with a mane and eyes of flame.

Rhyddhad had also shed her glamour, but I'd seen that on rides before now. It was the rest...I held out my arms to see black leather gloves running up to my elbows, and when I stared, the leather gave off a faint orange glow that writhed like flames.

Ricky rode up beside me and lowered his voice. "You okay?"

I nodded.

"Not going to speak?"

"Nope." My voice came out pitched a few octaves higher than usual.

Ricky laughed. "All right, then. We should probably get going."

I nodded, and Ioan waved to the others, telling them it was time.

FOUR

OLIVIA

THE HORSES stood at the edge of the forest. Deep within it, I heard the hounds. Ricky rode up beside me.

"They want us to lead," he said.

I nodded.

"You're okay with that?" he asked.

I should have been. I loved this part, as Matilda did in her time. I should have been chomping at the bit as much as the horses, eager to go, eager to hunt.

Yes, I knew this was no recreational gallop through the forest. This was *the* Hunt. Complete with human target. That would always be difficult. But this time was worse.

I had questions.

Questions Ioan could not answer. Questions I could not answer without halting the Hunt.

I needed faith. Ricky had it, resolve clear in the very set of his shoulders. Firm but not tense. Ready but not eager, either.

He trusted the Cŵn Annwn. So did I. More than I ever trusted the Tylwyth Teg.

So why did I hesitate?

Because I was part fae. Ricky was Ioan's grandson, and more than that, he was the true representation of Arawn. He fit into his role better than I did Matilda, better than Gabriel did Gwynn. Seeing him now, in that cloak, I had absolutely no doubt that Ricky *was* Arawn in every way that counted.

I wanted to be Matilda. For the Cŵn Annwn, I wanted to be her. That was what they needed and what I'd vowed to deliver.

"Liv?" Ricky said.

I motioned for him to ride in front of me.

"Pretty sure Matilda leads," he said.

"I'm being generous. But just this once."

He laughed, and it didn't matter if I sounded like a stranger. He heard *me*. He saw *me*.

That was faith.

"Go on," I said. "You've earned this."

I couldn't see his eyes, but I knew he was studying me. Trying to decide whether something was bothering me.

I plucked at the hood. "It fits weird."

He chuckled and then nudged his horse to the mouth of the path. I pulled in behind him. He lifted a gloved hand and counted down with his fingers. Three, two, one…

The moment Tywysog Du lunged forward, Rhyddhad was right behind him.

The horses tore along a path that should have been too small for them, one that would have brushed my shoulders if I walked it. But they whipped through like wind. That was what it felt like: riding the wind, the scenery blurring until it disappeared, even Rhyddhad seeming to vanish beneath me, no longer a creature of bone and muscle but one of spirit and smoke.

I loved speed. I had from my earliest memories of my father, Todd, whirling me around. As I grew up, nothing was ever too fast for me. Nothing was ever fast enough. Not a bicycle, not downhill skis, not even my adoptive father's garage full of classic sports cars. Only Ricky's motorcycle came close, but even that wasn't quite what I ached for.

Riding with the Hunt reminded me of high school and a boyfriend who I thought shared my love of thrill rides until I took him on the biggest roller coaster at Six Flags, and he declared that was too much. It crossed the line between exhilarating and terrifying. My first ride with the Hunt was like that, sitting behind Ioan. It was incredible, but it was also, perhaps, a little too much.

It wasn't just the speed. As Rhyddhad and I flew through the forest, I seemed to slip between dimensions or layers of time. There was no other way to describe it. She ran, and I caught glimpses of things that my brain couldn't even grasp. I heard impossible sounds and inhaled impossible scents. Some of them left me wanting to leap from Rhyddhad's back and track them down. And others made me hold on tighter, eyes squeezed shut, eager for them to be gone.

It wasn't like that for Ricky. To him, this was like riding the winding, sloping roads on Cape Breton, except doing it at double speed and never having to worry about crashing or losing control. He smelled, saw, and heard only the forest, and it was like crack to his Cŵn Annwn blood. The dimension-tripping was mine alone. My Matilda blood, reaching through time or memory, showing me more, whether I wanted it or not.

Since Ioan gave me Rhyddhad, I'd ridden enough that the experience no longer overwhelmed me. Again, it reminded me of that boyfriend, whose name I couldn't even remember. Within an hour, he wanted to try the roller coaster again. We went on it four times that day, and it never lost that edge of terror for him, but he came to enjoy it, like I enjoyed horror films, seeking them out even when I knew they'd give me nightmares. Riding Rhyddhad in her true form still terrified me, but it was the most exhilarating and complex experience imaginable, and so, when I rode that night, I was briefly able to forget my doubts.

When the horses caught up to the cŵns, they slowed. I leaned down to run my fingers through Rhyddhad's mane, seeing flame dance between my fingers. Fairy fire, without heat, without danger, endlessly fascinating.

The path widened, and Ricky waved me up beside him as the horses walked. In the distance, I could see Lloergan at the rear of the pack. They loped now that their prey neared exhaustion.

Johnson must have heard the horses behind him. He turned, and he stopped, and he stared. The hounds fanned out in a semi-circle, their heads lowered, growls rippling through the night air. Johnson didn't seem to notice them, though. His gaze was riveted to us. On the spectral horsemen and their flaming steeds.

"Who are you?" he shouted.

Silence answered.

"*What* are you?" he yelled.

"Judgment," Ricky called.

Yet it wasn't Ricky's voice or even the cloak-distorted version of it. It was Arawn's. I looked over, and that was who I saw from Matilda's memories. Arawn sitting ramrod straight on his steed. No sense of joy emanated from that figure. No excitement, either. Only the grim satisfaction of doing a job that must be done.

"Judgment for what?" Johnson said, his voice rising.

"Keith Johnson," Ioan said, his horse moving up behind ours. "You are guilty of the murder of Alan Nansen."

"Wh-what?"

Confusion rang in Johnson's voice. I told myself it didn't matter. I'd seen men and women break down sobbing in Gabriel's office, begging him to help, swearing they hadn't committed the crime… only to find evidence that they had. Evidence I tucked away because proving that wasn't my job. Before I tucked it away, I showed Gabriel, but only so he'd be prepared for what the prosecution might uncover. Even between ourselves, we never said that our clients were guilty. We knew they were, though. Most of them were.

So I should have heard the confusion in Johnson's voice and rolled my eyes. *Yeah, yeah, it wasn't you. You don't know this Nansen guy, and you have no idea what we're talking about.*

But I hesitated, and it had nothing to do with Johnson's pleas. His cries were only a reminder of what the ride had wiped from my mind. My own questions.

Ioan had said Keith Johnson murdered a man named Alan Nansen during a home invasion.

"Johnson killed a thief?"

Ioan shook his head. "That would be a justifiable act. We don't punish those who are acting in defense. Nansen was the homeowner."

Which meant that Johnson was the thief. A fifty-something, heavyset thief who drove a late-model Audi and dressed like a stockbroker.

Even as I thought that, I imagined Gabriel's snort. Gabriel, who knew how to pick a lock and wasn't afraid to commit a little B&E in search of answers. Gabriel, who drove a late-model Jaguar and wore custom-made suits.

The car and the suit meant nothing. Maybe Johnson was screwing the guy's wife. Maybe he was committing corporate espionage. Hell, maybe he earned that car and suit through his *career* as a thief.

So why was I hesitating? Did I look at this man and imagine Gabriel in his place, ripped apart by hounds because he'd broken into a house for information?

Except that wasn't this man's crime. Unlike me, Gabriel carried neither gun nor knife. He accepted the risk for committing a crime, and killing a homeowner to avoid arrest would never occur to him. While Gabriel didn't particularly care about the death of anyone outside his very narrow sphere, his own moral code stated that an innocent person should never die at the hands of someone committing a crime.

Keith Johnson had killed a homeowner while committing a crime. The deceased had fae blood. Therefore, Johnson earned this death, whether he knew it or not. Much like he would have "earned" a bullet from the homeowner if the man had been armed.

It was justified…if that's how it happened.

"Run," Ioan said, his voice startling me from my thoughts.

"What?" Johnson said.

"You heard me. Run."

"I haven't done anything—"

A growl from Brenin cut Johnson short. The big hound feinted…and Johnson ran. The cŵns gave chase, and Ricky followed. Rhyddhad danced beneath me, eager to be off but sensing my hesitation.

Ioan rode up alongside me. "You can skip this part, Liv."

The other Huntsmen thundered past in breathtaking blurs of fire and shadow.

"Your part is done," Ioan said.

"Pretty sure I haven't actually done anything yet."

His lips twitched. "Perhaps it wasn't quite as active a role as you're accustomed to, but it was enough. You rode with us. You heard the pronouncement. While normally Matilda leads…"

"I let Ricky. Just this once."

I smiled when I said it, but he studied me, knowing there was more to it. A reticence that did not become Matilda.

I straightened in my saddle and looked toward the baying of the hounds. "I'll lead next time. For now, I'd like to finish."

"You don't need to."

I glanced at him. "Is that a subtle way of telling me *not* to?"

Now he did smile. "No, just pointing out your options." He peered at me again and then nodded. "You're right. You should finish. Onward then. Let's see if you can catch up."

FIVE

GABRIEL

GABRIEL REACHED Cainsville just after eleven. He parked in front of Rose's house but then strode across the street to a three-story walkup instead, the only apartment building in the small town. Olivia used to live there. In fact, he'd first met her on the path beside it, last year when—

Last year.

It was almost exactly a year, wasn't it? He flipped through a mental calendar. Yes, it would be a year next week. He should get her something for the anniversary. Maybe a scone from the diner. Put it on her breakfast plate, and she'd arch her brows, and he'd say, "I owe you that."

It might take her a few minutes to figure out, but when she did, she'd laugh. They met in that passage when he'd waylaid her, trying to persuade her to sue for a portion of Pamela's book earnings. Olivia had shot him down. Then he'd pickpocketed the scone from her—a scone for her landlord, Grace—and presented to Grace as a gift.

So he owed Olivia a scone.

"It's about time," a voice snapped, and he looked up to see Grace herself, a boggart in a wizened old lady glamour.

Grace stood on the doorstep, her arms crossed, sunken-eyed glower on Gabriel.

"Taking your sweet time, Gwynn?"

He refrained from telling her not to call him that. One did not give Grace that kind of ammunition.

"Rose said you were out drinking. I presume that explains the smirk on your face crossing the road."

"I don't drink."

"Well, maybe you should start. Might help you deal with this." She waved inside her building. "Alcohol might help us *all* deal with this."

Gabriel fought a sigh. He'd done well, lifting his mood with memories of meeting Olivia. It couldn't last, though. Even before he reached the doorstep, he could hear Seanna screaming.

He tried not to wince, but Grace noticed, harrumphing as she ushered him in. "Never thought you were a glutton for punishment, Gabriel Walsh."

He glanced over.

"Oh, don't give me that look. You know how I feel about this. You need to stop coming when Rose calls. Better yet, Rose needs to stop calling you to come."

"I've told her to. Insisted on it. Rose doesn't deserve to bear the brunt of this. Nor do the fae here. It is a place of refuge for them. Of peace and rest." He nodded toward the screams. "That is hardly conducive to rest."

"She's like a baby throwing a tantrum. Ignore it, and she'll stop."

"Remind me how many babies you've raised, Grace?"

"One, actually. Which is more than you. More than Rose has, too."

He opened the stairwell door.

"Liv still doesn't know, does she?" Grace called after him.

He didn't answer.

"I should tell her. You know I should."

He turned and looked down the stairs at her. Just looked.

Grace crossed her arms. She didn't say anything, though. She knew better. Just as she knew better than to tell Olivia.

"I don't want to upset her," he said as he resumed climbing the stairs.

"Because she'll be so much *less* upset when she finds out you've been keeping this from her," Grace called up after him. "She will find out. You know that."

He kept climbing.

"For such a smart man, you can be a damned fool, Gabriel Walsh."

He walked through the stairwell door and continued on until it shut behind him. Then he paused.

Grace was right. Olivia would find out, and she would be furious. He'd fallen into this trap before. Over and over again he'd fallen into it. In the beginning, when he'd lied to Olivia or betrayed her, he'd told himself it was for her, when really, it had just been convenient for him. Gradually, that shifted, and he would do what he was doing now, not lying per se, but failing to tell her something significant because he really did hope to shield her.

One would think he'd have learned his lesson by now. He loved Olivia. He respected her. The absolute last thing he wanted was to damage their relationship.

And yet here he was, making another choice that could do exactly that. A damned fool indeed.

For two months, he'd been getting these texts from Rose, usually in the middle of the night. The first time, he'd been working downstairs while Olivia slept, and there'd been no reason to tell her he was leaving. Grace's apartment building was a five-minute walk from Olivia's house. So he'd left a note and slipped out. Then he returned, tossed out the note and decided Olivia didn't need to know about it. The situation would only upset and worry her, and for what? A one-time call in the middle of the night, a problem easily solved, with Gabriel back before she knew he'd left. No point in mentioning it.

When it happened again a week later, they'd both been asleep. The text hadn't woken her, so he slipped out, returned within a half hour, Olivia none the wiser. And there'd still been no reason to tell her—just a second random occurrence.

That "random" occurrence became a weekly routine, and by the time he realized it wasn't going to stop, he didn't know how to tell her. How to admit it had been going on for two months.

One of these times, she would realize he'd left. He needed to tell her before then. He'd been about to, a week ago, and then she got the message from Ioan that her first Hunt was coming, and Gabriel decided he couldn't add this to her stress. He'd wait until after tonight.

"I want *Gabriel*." Seanna's voice echoed down the hall, and Gabriel squeezed his eyes shut. Then he checked his phone, as if he might have an urgent message from Olivia, needing his help. As if he might have an excuse to flee.

Instead, he saw only Rose's text from an hour ago.

It's Seanna, again. I know Liv's off with the CA, and I thought if you were staying at her house, you might stop by. You don't need to, of course.

"I want my *son!*"

Gabriel gritted his teeth. He wanted to stride in there and tell Seanna to be quiet. No, he wanted to tell her to shut up. Shut the fuck up. Words he had never used in his life, even with the most difficult client.

Seanna was different.

Until a few months ago, he'd thought his mother was dead. Been glad that she was dead, and he felt no guilt admitting that. Seanna had made his early life quite difficult.

He heard Olivia's voice. *"Difficult, Gabriel, is when your mom makes you study from dinner until bedtime. Seanna made your life hell. Absolute hell."*

True, though he preferred "difficult." *Yes, yes, my mother was a drug-addled petty criminal who neglected me until I was fifteen, when she just walked out, but I'm past all that. Really, I am.*

He lifted his hand to rap on the door and saw it trembling. He squeezed a fist as anger darted through him. Anger and shame.

You will not do this to me, Seanna. You've done quite enough, and here I draw the line.

When the trembling stopped, he knocked. Three quick raps. Rose opened the door and, while she tried to hide her relief, he saw it in every line on her face.

This is why I am here. Not for her. For you.

"I'm sorry, Gabriel," she said. "I thought I could handle it this time, but she only got worse."

"It's no trouble," he said. "I was already on my way to Olivia's, and it was easy to stop by."

Rose bought the lie. Just as she bought the one he presented by walking in stone faced and calm.

A minor inconvenience, that's all.

Nothing to worry about.

"Gabriel," a voice whispered.

He looked down the hall and saw his mother. And it did not matter how many times they repeated this dance, each time he saw her, it was a blow straight to his stomach.

When Seanna abandoned him at fifteen, he didn't question her disappearance, never suspected foul play. That was the kind of mother she'd been, gone more than she was home, and every time he opened the door to find the apartment empty, he'd felt nothing but relief. When she disappeared for good, though, he'd realized that a permanently absent mother was an entirely different thing. He might be accustomed to working and stealing for his meals, but at least he'd had a home and an address for school.

When Olivia discovered Seanna had apparently died of a drug overdose all those years ago, Gabriel had again been relieved. Freed from his greatest fear—that after everything he accomplished, she'd return and blackmail him into giving her a share.

Then she *had* returned. The dead woman had been a setup, allowing Seanna to flee one of her endless bad decisions. She'd escaped and left Gabriel behind and saw no problem with that. He'd done well for himself, hadn't he? No harm, no foul.

He recalled the first time he saw her again, walking into the yard, lobbing insults at Gabriel, taking cheap shots at Olivia. And Olivia had laughed. With that, Gabriel had seen his mother for what she truly was. What she had become, in his adult eyes. A ridiculous and pathetic creature. He had outgrown his vulnerability, and she held no sway over him.

He defeated his bogeyman…and then Fate picked up the game board, flipped it over, and made him start again.

Olivia had discovered that Seanna had been marked as a child, taking from her that which separated humans from fae: their conscience. The Tylwyth Teg had removed the mark, which gave Seanna back her conscience. But undoing the mark would also give her back her memories, letting her know exactly what she'd done to her son. To keep her from going mad, the elders sedated her with fae potions and compulsions. At first, she had surfaced only in a state of semi-lucidity, like an elderly relative with dementia. That Gabriel could handle. But two months ago, she'd woken…and remembered she had a son.

"Gabriel," she said, and she walked toward him, her arms outstretched, and he longed to turn on his heel, walk out and slam the door.

Like hell, Seanna.

Do you think, for one second, that I am going to play this role? Let you play the one you denied me for thirty years? No. Now, good night.

That was what Seanna Walsh deserved. Yet this woman before him, frail and shaky, was not the Seanna Walsh he knew.

Did *she* deserve to have him walk out?

He didn't know. He couldn't tell how much of her was in there, and if there was little of the woman he knew—as Rose believed— then for his aunt's sake, he couldn't walk out.

Seanna's thin arms went around Gabriel, and he forced himself to pat her back, awkwardly, holding his breath.

Rose was quick to take Seanna by the arm and lead her into the room, saying, "Gabriel's coming in to sit with you. Don't worry."

Rose saw his discomfort. But she mistook it for simply the great-nephew she knew, who abhorred physical contact. This was different. For Gabriel, accepting a hug from a stranger was unpleasant, like an accidental shock—an experience not to be endured any more than necessary. A hug from Seanna felt like gripping that wire as tightly as he could. Unendurable.

Yet it had to be endured.

For Rose.

And for Olivia.

SIX

OLIVIA

I DID catch up. Well, Rhyddhad did. Once we reached the others, though, we slowed to a trot, and the world settled around me. As soon as Rhyddhad came up behind the last Huntsman, his horse instinctively moved aside. Without even a glance back, they kept giving way until Ioan and I were up behind Ricky.

"Ricky?" Ioan called above the thunder of hooves. "Let Liv go first."

Ricky nodded and moved his horse to the side.

"No," I said. "I'd rather—"

"Go," Ioan said. "Take the lead. That is your place."

I didn't *want* my place. Not tonight. Next time, I'd take it. Next time…when we had quarry that didn't raise so many questions.

But that was Ioan's point, wasn't it? That I needed to face this because I was uncomfortable with it, and the truth was that I wouldn't be more comfortable with any case. We could be chasing a drug-addled thug firing a semi-automatic over his shoulder, screaming, "Yeah, I did it, you motherfuckers!" and I'd be thinking he was too quick to take credit.

I would always question. So there was no point in waiting for next time. I had to make the leap. Lead the Hunt. Give the order. See justice done.

Watch Keith Johnson die.

I pushed Rhyddhad into the forefront. Then I called back, "What's the command?"

"For what?" Ioan said.

"To attack."

"There isn't one. The hounds will know."

I nodded. That helped—I wasn't sure I could form the words.

Ahead, the hounds were already closing in. They'd gotten Johnson deep into the forest; judgment had been pronounced, and all that remained was this final step.

Execution.

I am fine with this. I support this.

No, I was fine with the concept. I had to put aside specifics and accept that basic concept. Justice for fae. An eye for an eye.

I had seen a man killed by Lloergan. While I'd acknowledged extenuating circumstances—the whole situation was tragic—he'd confessed to knowingly murdering fae who'd been no threat to him. When he'd tried to flee, and Lloergan killed him, I'd regretted the way that it happened, but deep down, my Cŵn Annwn side accepted justice, harsh though it might seem.

I'd witnessed other cases, too, in Patrick's book on the Cŵn Annwn. I'd watched those scenes unfold, and I had been able to nod and say, "Yes, this is correct."

So hold onto that. If it was justified in every case I have ever encountered, then it must be here, too.

As I moved into position, Brenin surged forward. The other hounds fanned out, ready to cut Johnson off if he veered from the path.

He did not veer. He hunkered down, as if buoyed by how far he'd gotten, thinking he could still do this, could still outrun them.

Then Brenin leapt.

The alpha cŵn hit Johnson, and the man slammed face first into the ground. When Johnson flipped onto his back, Brenin lunged and pinned him.

But what if... The story... It doesn't make sense, and I need it to make sense.

Too bad. Too late. I should have investigated when Ioan gave me that option.

I am not okay with this.

But I would be. I had to be.

Get it over with. Just make the killing blow, and then I will leave, and I will work through the rest.

Brenin looked back at me. Our eyes met, and my stomach twisted.

He seemed to be awaiting a command. But Ioan said he didn't need one. He said Brenin would know what to do on his own.

The massive alpha just kept staring at me.

Just...just do it. Get it over with. I'll be okay with it. Eventually. Just—

Brenin stepped off Johnson. He continued backing away. The man rose, shakily. Johnson stared right at me. Then he turned and ran.

And the hounds did not pursue.

I spun on Ioan. "What the hell happened?"

"It was not the right time."

"Why?" I looked around. "We're in the forest. We brought him this far. You pronounced judgment."

I reached up to push off my hood, but it wouldn't budge. I ripped open the clasps, and the cloak fell onto Rhyddhad. A wave of dizziness hit me, and I nearly tumbled off the horse. Ricky grabbed my elbow.

"I did this, didn't I?" I said, my voice my own again. "I failed."

"What?" Ricky struggled out of his own cloak and let it fall as he rode forward. "No. You didn't *do* anything." He looked at Ioan. "Tell her she didn't do anything."

"She did not."

"But it's my fault they stopped," I said. "Brenin looked right at me. He needed something from me, and I didn't give it. You said there wasn't any command, that I didn't need to tell him..."

I trailed off and then looked at Ioan. "He sensed I had reservations. That's why he stopped. That's the command I need to give, isn't it?" I tapped my head. "Up here."

"No," Ricky said. He turned to Ioan. "If Liv was supposed to do or say or think *anything*, you would have told her that. You would never let her unintentionally sabotage a Hunt and then blame her for it. Because that would be a shitty, shitty thing to do."

"I'm not blaming her for anything," Ioan said, his voice calm.

Behind him, the Huntsmen had dispersed, giving us privacy. Johnson was long gone. So were several of the hounds, including Brenin.

"We can't just let him walk away," I said.

Ioan chuckled. "Oh, I believe he's running, actually. As fast as he can."

"*Hey,*" Ricky said. "This isn't funny. What the hell just happened?"

"I didn't have faith," I said. "Ioan told me what Johnson did, and I had questions, and Brenin sensed that. I wasn't sure, and so I completely fucked up the Hunt. Now we've got a guy who saw the Hunt and escaped. And it's my fault."

I slid from Rhyddhad and stalked into the forest. I heard Ioan say, "Liv," and start after me, but Ricky stopped him.

"Is that what happened?" Ricky said to Ioan, his voice ringing behind me. "You tested her—failing to mention that it *was* a test? That is a fucking shitty thing to do, and she did not deserve it. She is here for you. To *help* you."

"I know," Ioan said. "Perhaps I went about this the wrong way."

"Perhaps?"

"But I don't think I did."

Footsteps tramped after me. I turned to see Ioan approaching, Ricky bearing down on him. When Ioan stopped, Ricky swung past, walking up beside me.

"If you want to go, we're gone," Ricky said.

"No, I want to hear how the hell the leader of the Cŵn Annwn thought letting me screw up was a good idea."

"It was not a test," Ioan said calmly. "I knew you had questions. That was why I put you in the lead. To show that we will not do this *while* you have questions. If I'd insisted you investigate beforehand, you'd have refused. So I had to show you."

"At the cost of ruining a Hunt? Letting him get away to tell the world what he saw?"

"Hunts are *ruined* all the time, Liv. The circumstances aren't right or we're interrupted or we simply fail. Brenin will run Johnson until he collapses. Then one of my men will return him to his car. Johnson will wake behind the wheel, with a bump on his head to explain what he will mistake for a wild dream."

I headed back for the horses. "No. Let's get this over with. You said I didn't need to be there for the kill. So have Brenin bring Johnson around, and I'll hang back, and we won't have to worry about my lack of faith."

"As I said, no one expects you to have blind faith, Liv," Ioan said. "You aren't the only one with doubts here."

He looked at Ricky, who shrugged at me.

"Yeah, I do," Ricky said. "I didn't mention it because I thought that would make it worse for you. I don't doubt that this guy is guilty. My gut says he is. But does the punishment equal the crime? That's a whole other story. Unless you're a mass murderer, I don't think you deserve to be torn apart by giant hounds. But this guy doesn't deserve to walk around scot-free either. I'll accept this."

"I accept it, too," I said. "So we're good to go. Resume the Hunt—"

"No," Ioan said. "You are deeply uncomfortable with this, Liv. We've all seen that. You must get your answers. You must prove to yourself that Johnson is guilty."

"That isn't possible."

He frowned. "But that's what you do, isn't it? As an investigator?"

"Uh, no, I help set killers free."

The frown deepened. "What?"

"Gabriel is a defense lawyer," Ricky said slowly. "He keeps people out of jail. People like me. Like my dad. You do know what your son does for a living, right?"

Ioan waved that off. "You break laws. You don't commit murder. Or, I suppose, that might be naive. *You* haven't, Ricky. I would know otherwise. Whatever your father has done, it was in defense of others and *to* those who've chosen a similar way of life. That sort of crime doesn't concern us."

"But Gabriel…" I began. "Not *everyone* he defends has those excuses."

"It doesn't matter. That's human justice. If the court fails to find them guilty, they will still be punished in some way. That is how the world works."

I could point out that even the Cŵn Annwn couldn't punish every crime against fae, but I kept my mouth shut. If Ioan believed I only set people free to face a more cosmic justice, it was best to let him keep that illusion.

"The point," Ioan said, "is that you know if Gabriel's clients are innocent or guilty. You discover that in your investigating. That is what you need to do here."

"It's not that…" Ricky began. Then he saw Ioan's expression and stopped.

"It's not that easy," I finished. "I'm not sure I can ever say, with absolute certainty, that someone is guilty."

Ioan only smiled and patted my shoulder. "Of course you can. That's what you do, Liv, and you're very good at your job. Tonight's Hunt is over. Take a few days, investigate and prove to yourself that Johnson is guilty. Then Brenin will see that you are satisfied, and we can finish this."

SEVEN

GABRIEL

"HE'S RIGHT behind us," Rose assured Seanna, who kept glancing back as she was led into the living room.

Did Seanna sense Gabriel's urge to flee? It was possible—there had always been something feral in his mother, and while Rose might say that had been her lack of a conscience, Gabriel had gleaned enough from the elders to know she'd always had that, even as a child. A preternatural sense for trouble. A preternatural instinct for survival. Gifts of the fae, passed on to her son.

Rose sat Seanna on the couch and tried to take the spot beside her. Seanna made a noise, not unlike a dog's low growl of warning, and she reached for Gabriel.

"Gabriel can take the chair," Rose said.

"No, I want my son here."

"It's all right," Gabriel said, and he kept that mask firmly in place as he lowered himself to the sofa.

Seanna took hold of his hand, gripping it with ice-cold fingers.

"They wouldn't let me see you," Seanna said in her petulant-child voice. She aimed a glare across the room. "Rose said you were busy."

"I work in Chicago," Gabriel said. "My condo is also in Chicago. You know that. I cannot get here in an instant."

A crafty look lit her blue eyes. "So you were in the city?"

"Yes."

"Then you weren't with her. Is it over then? You've dumped the little—"

"I am still with Olivia. Very happily with Olivia. She is away this evening, so I was working late."

"I don't like—"

"Yes, you've made that perfectly clear."

"She's a spoiled bit—"

"I am well aware of your opinion of Olivia, and you are well aware that if you continue in this manner, I will leave."

His mother grumbled.

She saved your life.

He wished he could tell Seanna that. Wished he could tell her everything.

Olivia hated you—the old you—for what you did to me. She said she hated you the way she'd never hated anyone in her life. But when Pamela tried to kill you, it was Olivia who stopped her. The only person who cared enough to stop her. I didn't. That is the woman you despise, Seanna. Your guardian angel.

And *that* was why he couldn't tell Olivia about these visits.

She had saved Seanna for him. Because she knew that while in that moment he hadn't cared if his mother died, he also hadn't fully processed the news that she bore the mark of the sluagh. If he had turned his thumb down—voted for death and withdrawn from the room—he would have regretted it.

When it became possible to remove the mark, Olivia had supported this course of action. Take away the mark, return Seanna's soul and let her live out her days in a fae-drugged state.

"You don't ever have to visit her, Gabriel."

"Rose should not be saddled—"

"She won't be. I'll help out. So will the elders. They owe us."

"We'll see how it goes."

In the beginning, it played out as they anticipated. Seanna would wake, and Rose would tend to her. Gabriel and Olivia would visit, like visiting an infirm relative, one not entirely in her right mind. Some days were better than others, but mostly Seanna behaved herself. She took tea with them. Listened to them talk. Seemed to know who they were from visit to visit but occasionally needed Rose's reminder.

Then the night waking began.

If Olivia knew about these visits, she would realize why Gabriel sometimes woke not quite himself. Quiet and subdued, as if struggling with something, telling her it was simply a case weighing on his mind. Olivia would insist on witnessing these visits, and she would not sit there, like Rose, anxiously watching for signs that Gabriel was uncomfortable. One glance at his face and she'd know exactly how he felt.

"Do you remember when we used to go to the park?" Seanna said. "You loved going to the park."

He looked over, startled from his thoughts. Then he replayed her words and tried not to blanch.

Yes, I remember going to the park. I remember that you would drop me off and leave me for hours. More than once, you left me there all night. I believe that started when I was…four? Yes. Four or five, I believe.

"What did we do at the park, Gabriel?" Seanna asked. "I can't quite remember… There were swings, weren't there?"

"Seanna, maybe we should—" Rose began.

"Yes," Gabriel said, unhinging his jaw. "I went on the swings."

He did. He didn't actually swing on them, though. He never understood the attraction—Seanna didn't waste money on toys or waste time encouraging play. He did read, though, quite a lot, and that's what he'd do on those swings.

Gabriel could feel Rose's gaze on him. She knew Seanna wouldn't have played with him in the park, but she might accept the possibility that his mother had watched him play while she conducted business.

Olivia was the only person who knew the truth.

Seanna continued to prattle about parks, and deep in a corner of Gabriel's psyche, he could not help but wonder whether she was taunting him.

They had hypothesized that when Seanna regained her conscience, she would also regain her memories but that those memories would be weak, ephemeral. That did indeed seem to be the case. Seanna knew Gabriel was her son and that they'd been separated when he was a young man. She recalled wisps of their lives together, but if she remembered any of what she'd done to him, she seemed to dismiss it as nightmare. Her damaged mind playing tricks on her. Rose had told Seanna that she'd been in an accident. A terrible one that robbed her of her memories.

And so, to protect what remained of her sanity, it appeared that Seanna willfully chose what she would and would not remember. What she would and would not believe about her past. Instead of remembering that she'd abandoned Gabriel at fifteen, she seemed to think that Gabriel went off to college, and she'd taken a job in another state, and they'd drifted apart.

But now they'd been reunited. Mother and son. And she could not be happier.

"Did you bring me anything?" she asked.

He opened his mouth to say no. To make it very clear that she should not expect more than his presence. And perhaps to subtly hint that she did not deserve more. He had no desire to force Seanna to remember how she'd treated him—he saw no point in it—but he also saw no harm in distancing himself, in suggesting that their past relationship had been…strained.

Strained. There was nothing wrong with that. His relationship with Patrick was occasionally strained and always complicated, yet just because Gabriel would never truly consider Patrick his father did not mean they didn't *have* a relationship, even a decent one…at least for the time being.

Yes, a past strained relationship seemed the perfect way to resolve this problem. *You were not the best mother in the world, Seanna, but I'm here now, and I will support you. I am willing to come and to talk to you, and I believe that should be sufficient.*

Yet the moment he opened his mouth to say no, he had not brought her anything, Rose said, "Gabriel brought you a candy bar," and produced a Snickers from her purse. "Your favorite kind."

He had not, of course, brought it. Rose kept a stash of Snickers at home and always carried one in her purse, for just this occasion. He also suspected she sometimes gave Seanna one when Gabriel was not there, saying he'd left it for her.

"You don't need to do that," he said after the first time.

"It's a small thing, and it makes her happy."

He'd tried to pay for the bars. Of course, she wouldn't take the money. What he really wanted, though, was to tell her to stop.

Stop trying to make this all right, Rose.

I know you feel guilty. Guilty for what happened to Seanna, guilty for what happened to me. But you aren't. You didn't see what she became. I hid the worst of it from you.

He'd hidden the worst, and now he paid that price because Rose had no idea how deep the scars ran.

His phone rang. A bouncy little tune that made him smile every time he heard it. Smile inwardly, at least. Outwardly, it only made him grab his phone fast enough that Seanna noticed, and her eyes slit, jealousy oozing.

"Don't answer that," she said.

"Gabriel *will* answer it," Rose said firmly. "Don't speak to him like that."

"It's her. I know it is."

"It's not," he lied. "It's a client, and it must be urgent if he's calling at this hour. I'll take it in the hall."

He got up and strode out before she could respond.

EIGHT

OLIVIA

RICKY HELD the door as I walked into the bar. Gabriel wanted to pick me up rather than having Ricky drive me to Cainsville. I wasn't sure how much more convenient that was for anyone, but Gabriel had insisted. So we needed to kill time, and booze seemed like a very fine way to kill it.

We found a local bar on a local highway. Which meant it was full of locals, and I swore every guy under forty sat up straighter when Ricky walked though wearing his leather jacket with its distinctive Satan's Saints emblem. In the city, most people figured the jacket was just a fashion statement. At a bar like this, they knew better.

It wasn't just the guys who noticed him, either. Ricky was twenty-two, gorgeous and wearing a biker jacket. Add in the fact that he was funny, sweet and had an MBA, and he was the most ridiculously over-the-top romance hero come to life. Although, I suppose, in the book version, he wouldn't actually be a biker. He'd be an undercover cop posing as one. Either that or he *wouldn't* be such a nice guy. Depended on your taste in romance heroes.

I took the chair facing the wall, knowing Ricky needed his back to it, in case one of the guys in here thought he could impress his date by getting the jump on a biker. No one had made a move when we walked in, though. They just looked. Assessed. Took in the fact that he was with a woman. Ricky wasn't looking for trouble, so no one seemed inclined to change that.

A few people did whisper to their companions as we passed. It had been a year since my picture was first in the newspaper, the socialite heir to the landmark Mills & Jones department store, who turned out to be adopted, her birth parents Chicago's most notorious serial killers. I hadn't exactly lain low since then. I'd meant to. But then I met Gabriel, and our adventures found me in the paper far more often than I liked.

After we'd ordered, I checked my phone. "Gabriel will be here in about twenty minutes. Again, sorry about this."

"He can tell that whatever happened freaked you out, so he wants to come get you. You're upset."

I made a face. "I wish I'd known I could ruin a Hunt."

"Ioan should have told you. I understand that he thought a demonstration would be more effective, and he doesn't seem concerned about Johnson escaping, but he should have warned you. He knew you had doubts."

The server dropped off Ricky's beer and my Scotch.

He took a long drink and then said, "But Gabriel isn't the only one fretting lately. What's going on with you guys?"

"It's nothing," I said.

Ricky leaned over the table. "I'm not *looking* for signs of trouble, Liv."

"I wasn't—"

"And I'm just reassuring you. If something *did* happen, I'd be the first trying to get you two back together. You guys work. That's the way it is. The way it was always supposed to be. If I'm trying to get you to talk about a problem, it's because I'm hoping to help resolve it before it gets bigger."

He leaned back. "I know, that's silly of me. It's not like you guys ever tie yourselves up in knots worrying about things you shouldn't have done, things you should have said…"

"Yeah, yeah."

"Which is ninety percent Gabriel's fault. Watching him navigate personal relationships of *any* kind is painful." He paused. "Kind of amusing, too. But mostly painful."

"He's sneaking out at night."

Ricky's brows shot up.

"It's not that," I said.

"You mean he isn't sleepwalking? Because that was the first thing I thought. As for any other kind of 'sneaking around,' this *is* Gabriel we're talking about. One of the best things about being with you is that he doesn't have to go through all the trouble of figuring out how to get sex with zero personal involvement."

"Glad I'm good for something."

"You are, and he appreciates it."

I rolled my eyes and then sipped my Scotch. "I know he's not cheating on me. But I don't know what he *is* doing. He's getting up and apparently going out for a walk. It just started in the last couple of months, which means it isn't chronic insomnia. Even during the day, I walk into the room sometimes, and I can tell he's a million miles away—and wherever he is, he's not happy. He snaps back to himself as soon as I say anything. And then nothing's bothering him. Nope, nothing at all. Just lost in thought."

"Is it a case?"

"He says that if I ask, but cases don't bother Gabriel. If he's losing, that just means he needs to do better. Even if he loses, well, a perfect track record is an impossible goal, and therefore a loss is merely a warning to avoid complacency." I ran my finger down the glass. "I think it's Seanna. Visiting her."

"Does she say anything to him?"

"Not really. It's like visiting a very quiet five-year-old. Seanna sits there. I talk. Rose talks. Gabriel sips his tea. Afterward, he seems fine. He really does. But then there are these night walks, and I don't see any clear correspondence between the timing of those and our visits to Seanna, so I just..." I shrugged. "I don't know."

"You could follow him. You *are* a detective."

I shook my head. "If he needs time to himself, I don't want to be the nagging girlfriend, who bugs him to tell me what's wrong and then follows him to see where he goes."

"You're never that girlfriend, Liv. Have you tried waking up when he's leaving? Asking him what he's doing?"

"I did once. He just said he was going downstairs to work. And then he went downstairs and worked."

"So—" Ricky stopped and raised a hand, and I turned to see Gabriel.

He'd hesitated inside the doorway, as if fearing he might be in the wrong place. He *looked* like he was—not many people here in suits—but seeing that hesitation made my heart thud. Gabriel could stride into a biker bar or a frat kegger or a society cocktail party without batting an eye.

He caught my wave, and he made his way over just as the server brought our nachos.

"Look at you," I said as he took the seat beside me. "Two bars in one night. That must be a record."

"Seven," he said, shrugging off his jacket. "I believe my record is seven bars in one night."

Ricky arched his brows. "And how many drinks?"

"None, of course. One cannot pick pockets with unsteady fingers. The advantage to a bar is that one cannot protect one's wallet nearly as well with an unsteady mind."

He set mine on the table.

"How did you—?" I stopped and shook my head. "I don't want to know."

"Actually, you do. The problem is that you left your purse open when you last checked your phone. I'd suggest you return that and zip it."

"Speaking of picking pockets, did you get anything from Ms. Assistant State's Attorney."

"I did. It was quite a successful meeting."

"Not so successful for her, I'm guessing?" I said.

"In any way," Ricky said with a chuckle.

Gabriel shook his head. "I'm quite certain she wasn't expecting *that*. She simply hoped that I'd be eager enough for *that* to check my caution at the door. She gave me what I *did* want, though. More on that later. Tell me about the Hunt."

I did. As I spoke, his expression didn't change. Gabriel's expression rarely changes. It's all in those ice-blue eyes, which cooled with every sentence I spoke.

"That is unacceptable," Gabriel said when I finished.

"Exactly what I told her," Ricky said. "I'm going to have a talk with Ioan. He did this because he knows Liv won't accept anything on faith. She needs to see it, experience it."

"Hey, I can believe what someone tells me," I said.

They both turned to look at me.

"What? I can."

"Give an example," Ricky said.

"Last week, you had to cancel dinner because your dad needed you. Did I question that?"

"Not the same thing...at all. My point is that Ioan was trying to accommodate you. I get that. But the very fact that you question *everything* means you were never going to take him at his word when he said that guy deserved his fate."

"I trust Ioan. He's earned it."

"I don't mean you think he's lying—I mean you aren't completely convinced that the Cŵn Annwn method of determining justice is foolproof. He should have insisted that you check out the case beforehand."

"Agreed," Gabriel said. "Now, not only has he upset you, but you're going to need to do more than just 'check out' the case. You'll want to conduct a full investigation. On your own time, with no expectation of compensation. That is unfair."

"Lack of compensation isn't exactly my main concern."

His grumble said it should be. Then he asked, "What do you know about the case?"

"A guy named Keith Johnson broke into a house and killed the homeowner. That's all I have. Oh, and a license number for Johnson."

When Ricky looked over in surprise, I said, "I made a note of it."

"Proving that you planned to investigate," Gabriel said. "I will refrain from pointing out that I suggested you do this beforehand."

"Refrain," I murmured. "I do not think that word means what you think it does."

"As much as I dislike the way Ioan has handled this, I suppose it is better than having you investigate after Johnson is dead, which you were clearly planning to do."

"Look it up. Not investigate."

"You memorized his license plate, Olivia."

"Oh, I also have the victim's name. Not to change the subject."

"Totally changing the subject," Ricky said.

"Victim was Alan Nansen." I took a notepad from my purse and jotted it down.

"Home invasion, you said?" Gabriel frowned.

"Right."

Ricky stopped, his hand over the nachos. "You know the case?"

"I was asked to represent the defendant."

"Keith Johnson?" I said.

"No, Nansen's wife."

"That's some luck," Ricky said. "Well, for Liv, not the poor guy's wife. Though, all things considered, it's good for her, too. I'd snatch up that case if I were you. Might be the first time you represent someone who's innocent."

"All of my clients are innocent." Gabriel paused. "Except the bikers."

Ricky grinned. "Touché. Okay, some of your clients are innocent. But this is a case where you know it from the start." He looked at me. "Yeah, you have doubts. But I don't. When I looked at that guy, I just..." He shrugged and took a nacho chip.

"You can tell?"

Ricky shrugged again, conveniently munching on the snack so he wouldn't need to answer. In other words, he *had* felt that Johnson was guilty. The gut-level awareness that the Huntsmen had. He just wasn't going to press the point and make me feel worse than I already did about spoiling the Hunt.

Not just spoiling the Hunt.

Letting a killer walk free. Which I'd done before—deciding guilt and innocence was not my job. So why did it bother me to let Keith Johnson walk free?

Because stopping him *was* my job.

My job as Matilda.

"Olivia?" Gabriel said.

I reached for a nacho. "Ricky's right. You should take the case. The Cŵn Annwn believe Johnson murdered this guy, so the odds are in our favor. Strongly. Plus, it means I wouldn't be working for free."

"I turned it down last week."

"The fact that you never even came to me for a preliminary assessment means you rejected it out of hand."

"Yes."

I looked at him. "You're going to make me ask why, which suggests you're hoping I won't, which suggests there *is* a problem."

"Not with her case." Gabriel took a sip of his water. "Hers was too simple. She didn't require an attorney of my caliber."

"That means she's obviously not the killer, which puts Johnson…" I peered at him. "That isn't what you meant at all."

"How can you tell?" Ricky said. "He didn't even blink."

"Because he's trying to figure out how to tell me something I really won't want to hear."

"It was a clear-cut case of misidentification," Gabriel said. "The couple had a break-in two months earlier. They had several additional instances where Mrs. Nansen was certain she heard someone try the door while her husband was out. The police found evidence of footprints to support her theory. The Nansens were advised to buy a gun."

"Shit," Ricky muttered. "I don't like where this is headed."

"Precisely. Mr. Nansen came home unexpectedly early one night, and his wife shot and killed him. As I said, the case did not require a defense attorney. Her family is wealthy and wanted the best legal representation, so someone gave them my name. I explained that they did not require such an expense." He paused, as if realizing that might make him sound considerate. "It would have required a great deal of paperwork and was, to be honest, a very boring case."

"Tragic is the word you want there, Gabriel," Ricky said. "It's a *tragic* case."

"No, it was foolish and avoidable. Whoever counseled her to get a gun—without suggesting any training in how to use it—deserves the blame. I suggested that, should they care to file a civil case. Though I fear that would be pointless. Otherwise, our courts would be overrun by such suits."

"Wait," I said. "She shot her husband?"

Gabriel hesitated before saying, "Yes."

"Any chance she didn't actually pull the trigger?"

"No." He looked at me. "I'm sorry."

"Speaking of who counseled her to get the gun, could *that* have been Johnson?" Ricky asked. "You might have been joking when you said—"

"I never joke."

"All right. So let's say Johnson tells her to get a gun. Does that make him responsible for her husband's death? Seems kind of…"

"Harsh?" I said. "I suppose it depends on the circumstances. If there was some way that, in telling her to get a gun, Johnson clearly caused her to shoot her husband, maybe that would qualify? Ioan didn't say he actually shot Alan Nansen. He said he was responsible for Nansen's death. What qualifies as 'responsible' to the Cŵn Annwn?" I shook my head. "I'll find out, but in the meantime, we should see if Mrs. Nansen is still in need of a lawyer."

NINE

OLIVIA

THAT NIGHT, I dreamed of a Hunt. Of racing across the moor on a roan mare. Hooves thundered behind me as hounds bayed up ahead.

I am Matilda.

Mallt-y-Nos.

Matilda of the Hunt.

A stallion rode up beside mine, but I flung out a hand to ward it back. Calum's laughter rang before the wind snatched it away.

Not Calum. Arawn. Lord of the Otherworld.

My grin broadened.

It still felt like a dream. Like someone would wake me and hand me a pretty gown and tell me I was late dressing for the ball. For some girls, *that* would be the dream. A life of gowns and balls and dukes eyeing me like a brood mare in heat. A brood mare with land and a title.

I hated that life. Despised it with all my being. This was what I wanted. To ride. To hunt. To be with Calum, a boy from the village brought to work on the estate, my dearest friend from the moment we met and then…and then more than a friend. Much more.

An impossible situation. Resolved in a spray of magic, like something from a fairy tale.

A real life fairy tale, with real life fairies.

The Cŵn Annwn. The Welsh Wild Hunt. They found me, and they told me who I was, and they proved it when I'd laughed at them.

Matilda of the Hunt, with Calum as my Arawn. Fated to be together.

"Do you want to ride with us?" the Huntsmen had asked.

What a foolish question. Of course I did.

"So you choose us?"

Choose them over what? Over the life I had by birth, a life of titles and castles and endlessly boring lessons in how to be a proper wife? Never. I chose the life I had *before* birth. The life I had when I lived in Wales, as Matilda.

Calum fell back to let me take the lead. That was my place now, and that was as glorious as the ride itself.

Ahead, I could see the hounds pursuing our quarry. A terrible killer who had slaughtered a fae-blood girl. Violated and then murdered her. For that, he would die. For that, he *must* die.

When the hounds pinned their prey, the leader of the Cŵn Annwn rode up beside me. This was my first Hunt, and so he would render judgment while I bore witness. We continued riding until we neared the hounds.

"Hamish Stewart," the Huntsman said. "You are guilty of the murder of Agnes Fletcher."

"Hamish?" I said, my gut freezing as I struggled to see the man the hounds had captured. "That—that is… No, there's been some mistake."

My voice came out oddly, and I tried to push the hood back but found that I could not.

"That is my cousin," I said.

"He is guilty," said the Huntsman.

"He cannot be. I have known him since we were children."

"He is. Judgment has been rendered, and so he shall—"

"No!" Calum leapt off his horse and ran forward. "If she says this is a mistake, then we cannot do this." He stood in front of Hamish, arms wide to shield him. "We'll send him to trial. If he is found guilty, then he will be subject to the Hunt's justice. I'll speak to the magistrate myself. Tell me what evidence I can give them and—"

Hamish lunged at Calum. I shouted a warning just as my cousin struck my lover in the back. I drove my mare forward, and Hamish stumbled away. I saw the dagger in his hands. I saw blood on the blade. Then the lead hound pounced, and Hamish went down beneath it. I wheeled my horse to see Calum facedown on the moor, blood pumping from his back, and I began to scream.

~~~

I woke still screaming. Screaming and shaking. Gabriel's arms were around me, his breath in my ear, whispering, "It's okay. You had a nightmare. It's all right now."

"Memory," I gasped, heart pounding. "I had a memory. Of another Matilda."

He pulled me against him as he sat up in bed, and I curled up on his lap, my heart hammering.

"So," I said when I could find my breath. "I screwed up a Hunt tonight. I doubted Johnson's guilt. And just in case I wasn't worried enough about that? Matilda sends me a memory of another incarnation of her who doubted. Who stopped a Hunt...and saw her Arawn murdered by their quarry."

"Ricky's fine."

I looked at him. "You know that's not what the vision means. It means I set free a guy who is guilty. Who might go on to hurt someone else."

Gabriel paused. Then he said, "I once successfully defended a man accused of killing his wife, who went on to kill his second wife three years later. I have also successfully defended a woman who I knew was not guilty...and she killed a young couple drunk driving two months later. Then, once, I failed to successfully defend a young man who I was quite certain was innocent, and while he was in prison awaiting his appeal, he was murdered by another inmate."

"The moral of the story being that people die, no matter what?"

"Or that I'm cursed, and people around me die more often than is the norm, so if anyone else does perish because of Johnson, you can blame me." He paused. "Also, you might want to be extra cautious yourself. Get an annual physical. Drive a little slower..."

"Never." I reached up and kissed him before backing off his lap. "Okay, maybe I'm overreacting."

"No, I would only suggest that *Matilda* isn't sending you memories. Those memories are yours, like a walk-in closet, filled with vignettes for every occasion. You are worried about setting Johnson free, and so your subconscious selected a memory that confirmed your worst fears. If you *hadn't* doubted, you'd have remembered an instance where the Cŵn Annwn were mistaken."

"So you think that's possible?"

"Let's see. In the last year, I've discovered I'm a manifestation of a legendary fae king from Welsh folklore, and my client's son is the Lord of the Otherworld, and my investigator is the Lady of the

Hunt. Oh, also, my father is a hobgoblin who writes romance novels and my mother was an unholy bitch because she was corrupted by the living embodiment of darkness. At this moment, I believe anything is possible."

"I like 'unholy bitch.' That's progress."

"Yes, I'm learning to own my inner rage and resentment. In flashes. Very brief flashes."

I kissed him again, this time letting it stretch, my arms going around him as I crawled back onto his lap.

"You aren't asking me to distract you from the nightmare and help you sleep, are you?" he murmured between kisses.

"Possibly."

"I'm not very good at doing things for others. You know that, right?"

"I think you're getting quite good at it. But you can always use more practice."

～〜⌐

ALAN Nansen's wife—Heather—had retained a lawyer, but when Gabriel contacted her family again, they jumped at the chance to have him re-evaluate her case. As he'd said, they certainly could pay his bills. I'd run into her parents at fundraisers, and while they didn't travel in the "old money" circles of my family, they probably had a fatter bank account. Heather was their only child, and although the police seemed ill-inclined to charge her with anything, her parents felt impotent, and to them, the best way to support their daughter was to retain the best lawyer around, just in case.

For Gabriel to turn down their initial offer was a huge personal achievement. Fretful parents willing to throw gobs of money at him for a case that would likely never see charges laid. At one time, he'd have snatched it and found work to do, racking up billable hours, and then when the police decided against charging Heather, he'd have taken credit for it.

That was the old Gabriel. The guy who had amassed a small fortune before his thirtieth birthday, with nothing to spend it on, yet driven by the compulsion to keep growing his stockpile. Driven by the boy from the streets, who hadn't known where his next meal would come from, let alone how he'd ever realize his dream of law school. That boy could never look at his assets and say, "It's enough."

I don't think Gabriel ever *would* be able to say he had enough. He was learning other priorities, though, like having time off for rest and recreation. And he was learning that having money meant he could be pickier with his cases. He wanted one that intrigued him. That challenged him. The murder of Alan Nansen had been neither...until now.

We would meet with Heather later that morning. First, I researched the case.

Alan Nansen owned a restaurant. Eclipse was a bit trendy for my tastes, which translated to "I like it...but not enough to make dinner reservations three weeks in advance." Gabriel and I had eaten there once, and I'd been with my adoptive dad when the place first opened a few years ago.

Running a successful restaurant meant Alan Nansen kept late hours on the weekends, and whoever targeted the Nansen house knew that. The first break-in happened on a Saturday night while Alan had been working, Heather home asleep. The burglar had stolen her purse before something scared him off. Then came two attempted invasions, also on weekend nights. Neither effort was successful, and police speculated that the intruder realized the Nansens had upped their security and backed off. That would make sense the first time. But twice more?

And if the Nansens knew these attempts were coming on weekend nights, couldn't they have changed their schedule temporarily? That seemed wiser than buying a gun.

Then, nearly two weeks ago, Alan Nansen came home early. Under the circumstances, you'd think he'd call and warn Heather. Instead, he came home and walked into the bedroom, and she shot him.

I hated to agree with Gabriel that Nansen's death was more inevitable than tragic. That sounded callous. But given the way it played out, yes, there was an air of inevitability to it.

So once again I had questions.

Lots of questions.

TEN

OLIVIA

WE WERE with Heather Nansen. Anyone else might see her home and wonder what she'd done to piss off her wealthy family. It was a small house in a good neighborhood, one that would be out of reach for the average thirty-year-old, but definitely not what you'd expect given who her parents were. It made sense to me, though.

My house was twice the size of this one, but probably half the price, given the hour's drive from Chicago. I came into my trust fund a few months ago. Five million dollars. And the only thing I did with it was pay off my mortgage. Sure, I liked my designer footwear, but I'd been able to scrimp for an annual pair with my diner paycheck. I also liked fast cars, but my adoptive dad left me a garage of them, and I only used one. I wasn't particularly frugal, but I grew up with money, so I was just accustomed to it. Which meant that while I had some champagne tastes, my trust fund wasn't a winning lottery ticket to be spent indulging fantasies I couldn't afford before. So I understood Heather Nansen's choice.

Her house was exactly what a childless couple might need, no more and no less.

When Heather answered the door, she looked… Well, I don't know how someone was supposed to look two weeks after accidentally shooting her husband. On the way over, I'd thought about that. My fae blood meant that, like Gabriel, I suffered from an inherent lack of empathy. A voice had always whispered that I was a little bit cold, a little bit ruthless. I've thought about how that shaped me, growing up, feeling like I lacked something essential. I had looked at my adoptive mother, a renowned philanthropist, and I'd tried to develop that sense of goodness by immersing myself in volunteerism and charity work. Now, given that she abandoned me for Europe after the news about my biological parents—and doesn't intend to return—I had to wonder exactly how much of that philanthropy *was* innate goodness…and how much was self-interest, that her charity work gave her purpose and stature.

When I learned who my biological parents were, that seemed to answer part of my puzzle. If I lacked empathy, well, I had convicted serial killers for parents. Learning I also had fae blood finally silenced that voice. I had a friend who struggled in school until she was diagnosed with a learning disorder, and I remembered how relieved she'd been. That had baffled me—the diagnosis didn't cure her. Now I understood her relief. The diagnosis meant that she wasn't failing because she didn't work hard enough—she had a disability she needed to accommodate. That was what my lack of a fully formed conscience meant. I wasn't a heartless bitch—I had a deficit that I needed to accommodate, which I'd been doing all my life.

On the way here, I'd practiced. I was about to meet a woman who'd accidentally killed her husband. To prepare myself, I recalled my memory dream. I had been that Matilda, whoever she was. I had been madly in love with my Arawn. And I had caused his death. How had *she* felt?

Shattered. That was what I remembered. It was a brick thrown through a window, shattering her universe in an instant. His death would have broken her at any time, but having been responsible for it…? That was devastating.

I needed to be ready for that with Heather. For a woman who had killed the man she loved. Unintentionally but not even accidentally, not really—it wasn't as if the gun misfired. She'd made a mistake, like the Matilda in my memories.

Heather Nansen answered the door dressed in jeans and a blouse, no makeup, her hair looking clean but shoved back carelessly. No bags under her eyes, yet she moved slowly, as if exhausted. She met us with a forced half-smile and ushered us indoors.

"My dad wanted to be here," she said, "but I told him no. Just because he insists on paying the bill doesn't mean he gets to micromanage my case."

She led us inside, down a hall, into the living room. "Can I get you…?" she began and then trailed off with a look of blank confusion, like a robot that realized it should know the rest of that line but found itself unable to access the data.

"We're fine," I said.

She nodded. And then she just stood there.

Shock. That's what it looked like—she was a woman going through the motions. After nearly two weeks, I would think that would pass into grief. Like when my dad died. I spent twenty-four hours in full-out Olivia mode, taking care of every detail while my mother broke down. I'd proven I was my father's daughter, efficient and collected. Then, once I'd contacted everyone who needed to be told and written the obituary and spoken to the funeral director, I collapsed in a puddle of ugly-crying grief.

Was Heather Nansen still in efficiency mode? Taking care of all details? Or *was* this her grief, her way of handling it—moving forward while periodically shorting out?

I considered the possibility that Alan Nansen's death was not an accident. I had to. Even before I started working for a defense attorney, I loved mysteries. I wrote my master's thesis on Sir Arthur Conan Doyle. I'd grown up dreaming of "being a detective" the way other kids think of "being a rock star," as a fantasy so unattainable I never dared voice it. I grew up in a world where being a PI or even a police detective was not an acceptable career goal.

So I had to consider the chance that the woman in front of me killed her husband. It was the perfect setup. Stage break-ins when he wasn't home to witness them. Use that as an excuse to buy a gun. Then wait until he came home early one night and, *whoops, did I do that?*

But while I didn't see a shattered wife in front of me, I didn't see a relieved one either. Unless she'd masterminded the perfect murder… and then realized that she didn't feel as good about it as she'd expected. That she missed him.

Or that she might actually need a defense lawyer.

The problem with loving mysteries? I saw way too many possibilities.

When Heather hesitated, I said, "Can we start by taking a look at your security system?"

"Yes, of course. I have an evaluation. After the break-in, we upgraded our system, and then Alan hired an independent expert to evaluate it. I can make you a copy of the report."

"Thank you," Gabriel said. "But my investigator will still want to examine the system herself."

"If that's all right," I added.

"Certainly. I'll show you where it is, and then I'll copy that report for you."

ELEVEN

OLIVIA

GABRIEL'S INVESTIGATOR did indeed examine the system, as part of her ongoing education. Which meant that, while Heather was gone, I assessed the system...and then Gabriel assessed my assessment.

The verdict? That the system wasn't nearly as good as the Nansens seemed to think. It afforded the illusion of perfect security, but a professional thief would have little difficulty breaking in.

While the Nansens were certain that the same burglar had targeted them three times, Gabriel wasn't convinced of it. The property practically waved a neon Rob Me sign. The house was surrounded by mature evergreens that would have blocked the neighbors from view, but there was also an eight-foot fence. What kept it safe from prying eyes, though, also kept burglars safe from those eyes as they prowled.

Then there were the windows. So many windows. Being a single-story house, for proper security, they'd have needed to arm each window. Instead, the alarms covered only the doors, including the sliding one on the patio off the kitchen where the intruder had entered. That was on a separate system, which Heather explained was kept armed unless they were using the back deck.

"Alan worried that I'd forget to arm the house when I was home alone," she said. "The police said the patio door was the most likely spot for someone to try again, so we left that armed all the time. Alan... He worried."

Her voice caught when she said that, and she cleared her throat with a quiet, "Excuse me."

Gabriel opened his mouth. A look from me shut it. I knew what was coming. He'd been about to tell her to take a minute, his catch-all reaction to people experiencing any surge of emotion.

Take a minute.

It sounded thoughtful and considerate, and clients took it that way. But even from the first time he'd said it to me, I knew what it really meant.

Take a moment and get this over with so we can move on.

Heather was entitled to bursts of emotion, and he could just keep his mouth shut and deal with it. It wasn't as if she seemed in any danger of breaking down sobbing uncontrollably, unable to continue. She was already back on track, showing us how the alarm worked.

"And you had an intruder break in here," I said. "That was the first sign of anyone trying?"

She nodded. "It was strange, really. I slept right through it. Alan got home, and when he went into the kitchen for a snack, he felt a draft. It was March, so the wind blew right through. He looked over to see the door open. At first, he thought I'd left it that way, but then he saw the lock had been forced. He got me up, and we reported it."

It was strange, really.

True, but the way she said it seemed oddly flat. Detached. Though it *had* been a couple of months ago, and it paled compared to what happened two weeks back.

"The only thing taken was your purse?" I said.

She nodded. "I kept it over there." She pointed to a hook on the wall. "In retrospect, maybe not the best idea. Someone just needed to look in the patio door to see it. The police thought the intruder got startled and left before he could grab more, but really, I'm not sure what else he would have taken. That was an easy snatch and run."

"But then he came back."

She crossed her arms, and now she did look uneasy. "Twice. Which…"

"Seems odd?"

She nodded. "I guess since the purse was so easy, he could have decided he'd come back for more. But twice?"

"You scared him off, though."

"I'm not sure 'scared' is the word. The first time, he tried the front door, and as soon as I turned on a light, he took off. The second, I saw the new motion detector light up the backyard. I thought it was just a cat, so I didn't freak out. I was still awake that time, watching a show on my laptop. I looked out, and there were footprints. It was when we had that freak snowfall a few weeks ago."

"The police seem to believe it was the same person each time."

She nodded. "I think so. There were prints the other times, too. First through the back garden and then under the living room window."

"The same prints?" Gabriel asked.

"The police couldn't say that conclusively—the snow ones had melted, and the first set were less distinct. But they were the same size and seemed like the same tread." She crossed her arms again. "I'm sorry. I guess all this doesn't mean much, considering the intruder isn't the person who…who shot Alan. I don't mean to go on. It just…" She looked at me. "It feels like *he's* responsible, though I know he's not. I am. I just…"

She straightened. "Enough about the security."

"Actually, this *is* helpful," I said. "In a potential case, Gabriel would need to establish the situation. The fear that you were living under."

"I wasn't—" A pained smile. "I shouldn't say that, should I? Otherwise, how do you explain…?" She shook her head. "I *will* explain. But first, the problem is that we weren't living in terror. We were living in defiance."

She waved us into the living room, where we sat.

"We didn't think it was an intruder. Not your garden-variety thief anyway. I haven't told the police that. It wouldn't help my case. After the first time, we did wonder why he just stole my purse. It was almost as if someone wanted to spook us rather than actually rob us."

She settled into the chair, getting comfortable. "When the next attempt came, Alan and I grew suspicious. It really didn't seem as if someone was trying to break in."

"Just spook you."

She nodded. "Yes. And all three happened while Alan was at work. While he was *known* to be at work. The busiest nights of the week."

I shifted forward. "Can you think of someone who might target you? Anything you tell us will be kept in complete confidence."

A humorless smile. "You mean whether I was having an affair and our intruder was my spurned lover?"

"Not necessarily. Maybe someone was paying you undue attention. Things like that can escalate, from the point where you don't want to sound paranoid to the point where you regret not feeling paranoid enough."

"True. But no. There wasn't a spurned lover or rejected suitor or mystery stalker. This wasn't about me. It was about Eclipse."

"The restaurant?"

She nodded. "What did someone stand to gain by pretending to break in on Saturday nights? Getting Alan to stay home."

When neither Gabriel nor I said a word, she said, "My husband needed to be at Eclipse. Having him there ensured everything ran smoothly on the busiest nights of the week. He was the captain of the ship and the face of the restaurant itself."

"So you thought someone was trying to make him stay home on the busy nights. To damage the business?"

"I know it sounds ridiculous, but restaurants are cut-throat operations. Most close in less than a year. Even one as successful as Eclipse wasn't exactly running in the black."

Gabriel met her gaze. "You are telling me that you feared a competitor was attempting to sabotage a failing business?"

She visibly bristled. "Eclipse isn't failing, Mr. Walsh. That's how newer businesses operate. How long did it take you to break even with your law firm?"

"Two months."

Her mouth opened. Then it closed.

"These are questions a prosecutor or the police could put to you," I said. "You need to be prepared."

She eased back. "Yes, of course. I'm sorry. In the restaurant business, it may take years to break even, and the chances of it ever being wildly successful are slight. It's a labor of love. A chance to live a dream. Putting Eclipse out of business means another restaurant gets those patrons and increases its own chance to survive. Having

Alan stay home on the busiest nights could be catastrophic. Which is why he insisted on continuing to work."

Gabriel said nothing for so long that Heather began to squirm and shoot glances my way.

"All right," Gabriel said finally. "I will accept that someone might have been harassing you in an effort to convince your husband to stay home. But if you suspected it *wasn't* an intruder, why did you shoot him?"

Heather jerked back as if slapped. She stared at Gabriel. Then she looked to me, waiting for the "good cop" to jump in. I met her gaze with a level stare. And I waited.

"I..." She hesitated and then inhaled. "I panicked. We told ourselves it was sabotage. Alan was so sure of it. But he"—another breath—"he didn't have to be here alone, hearing someone outside and hoping—praying—it was just someone trying to spook us. And then, when it happened, the way it happened..."

"Can you tell us about that?" I asked.

She nodded. "It was just before midnight. I was in bed—I'm not a night owl. I was asleep when I heard someone in the house. I got up and took out the gun. That was my plan. The next time this joker tried something, I'd scare the crap out of him. So I got the gun, but before I could even get out of bed, I heard footsteps running down the hall. Running toward our bedroom. The door flew open, and I saw a figure in the doorway and...and I fired."

"Without considering that it could be your husband?" Gabriel said.

She tensed at that. Not bristling now, just tensing.

"Yes," she said. "And I will never forgive myself for that."

"YOU don't like her story," I said as we got into the car.

Gabriel started the Jag and reversed from the drive. When he was on the road, he nodded at me. Telling me to go first.

"Alan was the one who convinced her it was a saboteur," I said. "Whatever she might say, she wasn't as sure. He tells her it's just someone trying to spook her, but meanwhile, I think she's kinda pissed. His explanation gave him an excuse to go about business as usual while she stayed home and prayed it wasn't a *rapist* looking for his opportunity to break in."

"I agree that she wasn't convinced it was sabotage."

"And she doesn't strike me as the kind of woman who'd be comfortable admitting she was afraid. That can be tough. If a woman says she's worried, the guy might brush it off, tell her she's overreacting. So let's say Heather believes she might actually be in danger. Then there's someone in the house, bursting into her room, in the dark, without any warning, not a text, not a call… If Alan thought he could do that—knowing his wife was armed—then I'm sorry, but he was an idiot. Not an idiot who deserved to die but…"

"Tragic mistake then?"

"It sounds like it, but…"

"You aren't convinced."

"No. I want to be, but I'm not."

Gabriel turned the corner. "Neither am I."

TWELVE

GABRIEL

OLIVIA STOOD at the floor-to-ceiling window, naked, close enough to the glass that she almost had her nose pressed against it. Gabriel walked in with two tumblers of Scotch in one hand. He set one tumbler on the end table beside her. As it clicked down, she said, without turning, "Yes, I still love the view."

"It's one of my favorites, too."

She looked then, as if she had to be sure he wasn't referring to the skyline. She smiled and picked up the tumbler. After a sip, she lowered herself to the floor, still at the window. They'd bought a new couch and moved it closer to take advantage of the view, and he settled on that, but she still needed to be closer, endlessly fascinated by the night skyline, fifty-five floors above the city.

As he watched her, he enjoyed a few minutes of undiluted contentment with a hint of satisfaction. This was what he'd wanted. *This* view. Olivia at his window. And yes, Olivia naked at his window, her skin glowing with sweat from sex. But even more than that, he wanted the expression on her face, reflected in the glass. Her happiness. *Her* contentment. Six months together, and if anything had changed, it was only for the better, as the early awkwardness and worry faded. She was still here, still happy, sitting at his window, enjoying his view.

One word in that statement, though, niggled at him. His. *His* window. *His* view. Half a year as a couple, and there remained a clear delineation between her home and his, and Gabriel wasn't quite certain what to do about that.

Shortly before Olivia and Ricky broke up, she'd said something that made him worry they might be moving in together. That was the sign he'd been watching for: that they would make their joint living arrangement official—"moving in" together in a more permanent way. Once they crossed that threshold, marriage would become a very real possibility, and Gabriel's own hopes would evaporate.

But it never came to that. As Olivia later said, what she had with Ricky was "in the moment." They were very happy together, but neither of them saw a future to it. Which had been exactly what Gabriel had wanted to hear.

Except now *they'd* been together for six months, and Gabriel wanted more. A seal of intended permanency. A guarantee was impossible, but he needed a sign that Olivia did see this as a long-term relationship, one that might culminate in marriage, though he did not require that, as long as the intent was there. The intent to form a partnership with a future.

A clear signal that she planned to stay with him.

Even thinking that made him twitch—the idea that he required such a thing. No one had ever accused him of a lack of ego, and that ego should hold him confident in the belief that Olivia should want to stay with him. That he was worth it. And if she did not agree?

Then he was better off without her, and he would accept her decision with equanimity.

Which was a lie. Perhaps the biggest he had ever told.

Gabriel was afraid Olivia would leave him. While part of that was Gwynn's old fear, Gabriel needed to admit to himself that there was more to it.

If anyone had dared suggest that he feared abandonment after Seanna's departure, he would have laughed. His mother had never truly been present in his life, and he'd grown up with only the most transient of friends and even more transient lovers. He was not the least bit concerned about losing people. He didn't *want* them to stay.

Which was the clearest proof that Seanna had left scars. She had raised Gabriel not to form attachments of any kind. Not to care if anyone left. Not to let them get close enough for him to miss them when they disappeared from his life. Better yet, he should leave *them* first.

Now that he had someone he didn't want to lose? He was terrified.

The problem was that he had no idea how to take the next step, no more than he'd known how to take the first one. He'd tried, but ultimately, the ball had been shunted to Olivia's court.

He couldn't ask her to move in with him. First, that implied giving up her house in Cainsville, which neither of them wanted. Even if he clarified that it did not, the question seemed rather ridiculous.

"I'd like you to move in with me, Olivia. Part-time, of course. When we aren't at your house."

"Uh, isn't that what we're already doing?"

He couldn't even make a symbolic gesture, like giving her his key or his security codes or closet space. They had exchanged keys and codes before they got together. The "guest room" in her house had been his from the moment she'd moved in, and she'd already been keeping toiletries and clothing at his condo for when they worked late together.

How did you start living together when you'd practically been doing so even before you began dating?

It seemed that the only solution was to skip that step and jump to the next. But if they'd never even discussed marriage, he could hardly present her with a diamond ring.

So bring it up. Start there, with the discussion.

I've been thinking.

He opened his mouth to say that…and nothing came out.

I've been thinking.

Just say it.

Olivia turned. "Can I ask you something?"

Gabriel exhaled in relief. "Of course."

She walked to curl up on the other end of the couch. "It's about Seanna."

He tried to hide his reaction, but she saw it and said, "I know, that's the last thing you want to talk about."

Yes. "No, of course not."

"Liar." She tucked her legs under her. "You hate me bringing her up. I hate bringing her up. I'd rather just"—her hands fluttered—"put her in some alternate reality. Like Grace's building really is another dimension. We go in, we talk to Seanna, we leave, and we forget all about it. *Poof.* She's gone. But it doesn't work like that. She stays in here." Olivia tapped her head. "But mostly," she said, gesturing to his head, "in there."

She met his gaze full on. "I know what's going on, Gabriel. What you're not telling me."

His breath stopped, and his heart hammered, hand tightening around the glass he'd forgotten he was holding.

She knew, and realizing that, he also understood what he'd really been doing as he'd watched her at the window and tried to figure out how to bring up the subject of living together.

Closing the deal.

That's what it was about. Locking her in. Erecting the barriers that would keep Olivia from fleeing if she found out he'd betrayed her trust…again.

I need to tell you something, Olivia.

Those should be the next words out of his mouth. Beat her to it. Confess before confronted.

And if that wasn't what she was about to say? Too bad. Confess anyway. It was the right thing to do.

Ah, yes. The right thing to do. Admit to the hell he was enduring…so Olivia could blame herself for letting Seanna live, for supporting her staying in Cainsville.

If he confessed, was he doing it for their relationship? Or for himself?

"What am I not telling you?" he asked carefully.

She untucked her legs and crossed them instead. "How difficult it is for you, having her in Cainsville. Visiting her. It's not a case keeping you up at night. I've seen you sleep like the dead the night before trials that have me in knots…and I'm not the one defending the case. This is about Seanna."

No, of course not. Everything's fine. Just fine.

"Yes," he said. "I'm…struggling."

Olivia leaned over and hugged him. "Thank you."

"For struggling?"

"Ha-ha. For admitting it." She settled in again. "Okay, so we've established the issue. Now for the solution. I'm going to make a suggestion." She looked up at him. "Take a break."

"From…?"

"Seeing her. Let me do it. I'll go to tea with Rose. I doubt Seanna will notice you're not there. I'm not sure she even remembers you between visits."

Oh, she remembers me.

"We could both stop going," he said.

Olivia shook her head. "No, Rose should have help."

"There are others who could do it. Veronica has offered. So has Pepper. It doesn't need to be you, Olivia."

"Yeah, it kinda does." A moment of silence, her gaze shunted to the side before she came back with, "But it doesn't need to be *you.* Anyway, visiting Seanna doesn't bother me. I consider it my good deed for the week. God knows, my account needs more of them."

Gabriel's fingers tapped the side of the sofa, and he stayed silent for as long as he could manage, which was about five seconds.

"I know you're joking, Olivia, but it's a serious matter. If you are the least bit bothered by visiting—"

"I'm not."

"If there is any chance that you are doing it out of misplaced guilt—"

"Nope, there isn't. It's an opportunity for me to have tea with Rose. There just happens to be this other woman, who is barely there at all. So it's all good." She rose and picked up her tumbler, draining it. "Now that's settled, and it's well past bedtime. Well, *my* bedtime at least, though I'm hoping you'll join me."

"Of course."

THIRTEEN

OLIVIA

AFTER THE office the next day, I could hear Gabriel in the adjoining room, where he met clients, which was exactly what he was doing. Only the low rumble of his deep voice penetrated the thick walls, but I could hear the client perfectly well as he demanded Gabriel defeat the evildoers who dared try to imprison him for a crime he...well, a crime he'd committed. But he'd had his reasons, by God, and who were these plebeians to question the reasons of a man of his stature?

Gabriel excused himself, and a moment later, the door to his office opened as he stepped in, closing it behind him.

"Politician?" I said.

"Hmm."

"How much is he offering?"

"Not enough."

"What did he do?" I asked.

"Electoral fraud."

"Boring."

"I thought so." He sat at his desk. "I came in here to check my schedule and see whether I can fit him in."

"Doesn't look like you can."

"Terribly vexing." He glanced at me, lying on the chaise lounge. "Are you all right?"

I put a hand to my forehead. "No. Defeated, I have collapsed on the fainting couch, to softly cry, 'Woe is me.'"

"Didn't find anything useful on the Nansen case?"

"Not a damned thing. Terribly vexing."

He walked over and sat beside me. "And by not finding anything, you mean no connection between the Nansens and Keith Johnson?"

"Exactly." I straightened. "I'm lost here, Gabriel. If Johnson walked in today, asking you to represent him, I'd say hell, yes. Take the case. Because I cannot even fathom how the police would have enough evidence to *charge* him let alone convict."

"Yet you are being asked to convict."

"I am, and that's the problem. I'm not being asked to defend or prosecute. I'm being asked to judge with no prosecution or defense arguments. *Here's this man. We believe he is responsible for this other man's death. What say thee?*"

I shook my head. "I screwed up, Gabriel. I agreed to help the Cŵn Annwn, and I thought I understood what that meant, but I didn't. I really didn't."

"You couldn't. Not until you had a case like this, one where guilt isn't obvious. Where it isn't even apparent."

"So what do I do?" I slid off the lounge. "No, sorry. I won't ask you that. My mess, my decision."

"Your decision. Not your mess. It's everyone's mess, including mine. Like you, I presumed that if the Cŵn Annwn saw guilt, then their quarry was guilty. That they bore the most elusive of judicial devices: a foolproof lie detector."

I looked at him. "Maybe they do. They're supposed to, and I have no proof that they *don't*. Yes, Heather is the one who pulled the trigger, but there was another party involved. Someone who put the pieces in motion. And if Johnson did that with malicious intent, and the result was that an innocent woman now has to deal with having murdered her husband? Then I'm not going to split hairs over the quality of justice. The Cŵn Annwn say they know Johnson is responsible. There is no evidence to the *contrary*. Therefore, I—"

A rap at the door.

"Yes?" Gabriel said.

Our office administrator, Lydia, walked in.

"Let me guess," I said and motioned toward the meeting room and the abandoned politician.

Lydia shook her head and shut the door. "I just received a phone call. Heather Nansen has been charged with murder."

AN hour later, we were in a police station, sitting across from Heather Nansen.

"I did not kill my husband," she said.

Gabriel didn't reply. He just sat there, his gaze on her, his face expressionless. Under that stare, she squirmed at first. Then her cheeks blossomed red, in humiliation and anger as her dark eyes blazed her thoughts.

You asshole. You cold-blooded son-of-a-bitch.

I wanted to jump in and play good cop, and I don't know whether that was to make her feel better or to defend Gabriel, but I did neither.

Finally, she said, slowly, "I did not *intentionally* kill my husband."

Gabriel nodded. "Good."

She found a humorless smile. "Because it's easier to represent the innocent, I'm guessing?"

"No, actually, it is not. The stakes are much higher with an innocent client, which makes such cases more difficult. When I said 'good,' I was referring to your change in phrasing. Obviously, you don't need to be reminded that you *did* pull the trigger, and it seems cruel to do so, but that is exactly the trap you will find yourself in, whether it is with the media or the prosecution. Language matters, and they will be quick to jump on improper wording, and thereby get exactly the reaction I just did, one that does not make you look like an innocent woman."

She flushed. "Okay. I'm sorry."

"No need to be. I was demonstrating a point."

"So, look in the mirror and repeat 'I *did* kill my husband' fifty times?"

"I think it would be more useful to repeat 'I did accidentally shoot my husband.'"

"I was joking."

"I'm not. You must allow yourself to react to the reality of what has happened without allowing yourself a defensive position. The law is not your enemy here. It is the ally that will permit you to hold your head up and say that a jury of your peers agreed you committed only a tragic error."

She nodded.

"Now, you have already given me one account of that night's events. In light of this new evidence, perhaps you should rethink that account."

Her cheeks flamed again. "I told you the truth."

"Excellent. Then you will get up on the stand, and when presented with evidence that you summoned your husband home, you will simply say, 'I did not.' Ask for a stack of Bibles, too, so that you might swear on it. That helps."

"I know you're mocking me, Mr. Walsh, but that *is* all I can say. I didn't send those texts the police found on Alan's account."

"Then we need to prove it. Otherwise, swearing on a stack of Bibles is your best hope, and I'll warn you, I've never seen that actually sway a jury. Now, you told me that you had no idea why Alan returned home early that night or burst into the room without warning."

"Yes."

Gabriel lifted a sheet. "11:09 p.m. You text Alan 'Someone's outside the house.'"

She opened her mouth to respond, but he raised a finger and continued. "He replies to you, telling you to call the police. You say that you already did, but they don't have a car in the area, and you think they're ignoring you. You beg him to come home. He agrees. Then, at 11:40, as he's pulling into the drive, you text again, 'Someone's in the house!' He says he's on his way in. One final text 'He's coming into the bedroom!' Which is presumably when your husband threw caution to the wind and raced in to save you and..."

"I never sent those texts."

"Then your cell phone number isn't—"

"It's my number," she said. "But I didn't change it after my purse was stolen *with* my cell phone in it. Whoever stole it must have sent those texts."

"You believe someone sent those texts from your old phone and they appeared on your new one? That isn't how technology works, Ms. Nansen."

"Then I was hacked."

"Conceivably."

She relaxed in her chair. "Thank you."

"And these messages never appeared on your phone?"

She shook her head.

"Nor on your husband's?"

"I wouldn't know—"

Gabriel cut her off by pulling another page from his folder. "At the time of his death, Alan wasn't carrying his cell phone. The police asked for it, and you said if it wasn't in his pocket, then he must have put it down. According to the police, a brief search did not reveal the whereabouts of the phone, and you were too distraught to assist. You located the phone the next day and asked whether they still wanted to see it."

"Yes, they said they would send someone by for it, but they never did. Presumably, they didn't see the point. If you're implying that I would have read those messages on his phone, I don't have the passcode."

"No?"

"No."

"So if I ask to see his phone, you will produce it, and I will confirm that it has not been accessed since his death? Good. I will suggest that you present it when the state's attorney is also present, so that we might both confirm—"

"Yes."

His brows shot up. "Is that yes, you will do this? Or yes, you are admitting that you saw these texts?"

Her cheek twitched. "I did not send Alan those texts, Mr. Walsh."

"As you have said. The current question, however, regards *see-ing* them, not *sending* them. The police are at your house now, where they will either find your husband's phone or wonder why they cannot. They have yours already. Even if you have erased the messages—"

"His phone was still in his hand when he...when I..." She took a deep breath. "It was in his hand. He dropped it. I grabbed it to call 911, and I saw the last text, supposedly from me. I panicked. I had no idea what was going on, but in that moment, I knew I was in trouble. So I hid his phone, and I called 911 on mine. I checked my texts, and they were there somehow. I deleted them on my phone and on Alan's, and then I hid his until I had time to confirm they were gone."

FOURTEEN

OLIVIA

"IT'S THE perfect recipe for murder," I said as Gabriel drove back to the office.

"Is it?"

"Hell, yeah. Stage a break-in where the only thing grabbed is your purse, conveniently containing your phone. Stage two more attempted break-ins. Convince hubby that you don't need him to stay home—you just need a gun. Then, text him in a panic, luring him home. Shoot him. Delete the texts, and if they're discovered, well, they obviously came from your missing phone."

"Hmm."

I glanced over at him. "You disagree."

"I take issue with the descriptor 'perfect,' which I know you meant as hyperbole, but as murders go, it's far from perfect."

I considered and then thumped back in my seat. "Agreed. There are too many ways this could have gone wrong. All it would have taken was for Alan to call the police himself. Or send someone else to check on her. It's clumsy. The type of murder that seems clever only because it worked out as planned."

"Which describes ninety-five percent of murders committed by amateurs…and far too many committed by professionals. It's only when the plot fails that we see the flaws."

"And then we say 'well, that was a stupid idea.' Okay, so if Heather did this, she's no mastermind. She's just lucky."

"Yes." Gabriel turned a corner. "However, I don't believe our prime objective is to prove she did it, not as her defense team…or Ioan's prosecution team."

"Right. We know the Cŵn Annwn think Keith Johnson is responsible. That gives us a head start on an alternate suspect. Which would be a lot more useful if I could find any possible motive for him killing Alan Nansen."

"Hmm."

I glanced at him. "That noise means you're avoiding stating the obvious. That motivation isn't the starting point. Not even the ending point. I need means and opportunity. *Could* Johnson have done it, rather than *why* he would."

"Not him specifically. Step back to the general."

"Could anyone else have done it? Pulling the trigger, no. Heather admits she did that. If anyone else is responsible, it's the person who set this in motion. The one who staged the break-ins. The one who presumably sent the texts."

"Yes."

"I know texts—like phone calls—can be spoofed to look like they came from another number. I don't know whether that would explain the delay in showing up on Heather's phone… Wait. We need access to all her past messages. I can analyze her texting patterns. That won't prove conclusively that she didn't send them but—"

Gabriel handed me the folder. I opened it to find transcripts from Alan's cell phone, specifically the thread of his regular text conversations with his wife. I only had to skim through a few elements—word choice, abbreviations, emojis—to let out a curse.

"Yes, they match," he said.

"But this *might* be the real reason her cell phone was taken. To imitate her texting patterns, to convince Alan that it was her."

"That is more likely."

I returned the pages to his folder. "Three scenarios. First, no one ever tried breaking in, and Heather staged it all. Second, someone did try breaking in, and Heather took advantage of the setup. Third, everything was staged by an external party, who either knew she had a gun or..."

I considered. "No, I don't see any other explanation. The only reason that the third party would summon Alan home with those increasingly frantic texts is if he knew Heather was armed. It's still far from foolproof. Like, a hundred miles from foolproof."

"Just because *you* see that doesn't mean a third party would. It's tunnel vision. He has set up his pieces, and he sees only the play that he intends."

"Or he's just not vitally invested in success. He's taking a chance. How to commit murder without being tied to it in any way. That's some trick."

"One that must come with the risk of failure. Significant risk."

"And it did pay off. Alan is dead."

"With Heather charged in his murder."

I glanced over at Gabriel. "Which isn't an incidental outcome, is it? This was staged so Heather would pull the trigger. So she would accidentally murder her husband. But she wasn't about to be charged, and the police weren't looking for any other suspects. Case closed. Yet someone didn't want it closed. The police got a tip on the texts, didn't they?"

Gabriel nodded. "An anonymous call from a person who claimed to work at the restaurant and knew text messages had summoned Alan home."

~~~

MY theory was that Keith Johnson made that call. I had to dig deeper into the man himself.

My preliminary work revealed no obvious link between Johnson and the Nansens. Johnson was ten years older and hadn't gone to school with either of them. He was actually from New Jersey, and had moved to Chicago five years ago when he married. After his wife had died two years ago, he'd stayed, having settled into a job and a home.

As for his job, I'd shamed my profession by jumping to a conclusion based on circumstantial evidence. Johnson was a middle-aged guy wearing a good suit and driving an expensive car. Ergo, he must be a successful professional, maybe a doctor or lawyer or stockbroker. But there was at least one career that would explain the suit and car *without* necessitating a six-figure salary. Car salesman.

Johnson worked for a local Audi dealership. The car belonged to them—one of his perks. The suit exceeded his budget, but he wore it for the same reason Gabriel had begun wearing tailor-made suits before he could afford them: they made him look successful.

I'd thought maybe that was the link—that Johnson had sold the Nansens a car, which established a connection, maybe an infatuation with Heather. But the Nansens drove a Land Rover because Alan Nansen's brother-in-law owned a Rover dealership. Even that tenuous link didn't mean anything—the two dealerships were at opposite ends of the city, in no competition.

Research wasn't getting me anywhere. I needed to talk to Johnson…and pray Ioan was right, that Johnson remembered nothing of the night he'd been hunted by giant hounds and hooded horsemen.

FIFTEEN

OLIVIA

I SWANNED into the dealership where Johnson worked and tugged off my Versace sunglasses.

"Hello?" I trilled. "Can someone help me? I need to buy a car."

A few heads turned, just bemused glances at first, no one exactly rushing from their offices...until they saw me. Then a tsunami of salesmen rolled into the showroom.

I wasn't exactly a supermodel, but when you're twenty-five and blond, sometimes that's all you need. In this case, that was only half the package. The rest was the outfit. Start with the sunglasses I'd snagged from my parents' place where I'd left them. Great specs, but they really did scream "spoiled socialite," and that wasn't the image I liked to project...unless I *really* wanted to project it. Take the sunglasses, add knee-high boots, leggings and a flowing scarf, and I was screaming spoiled socialite at the top of my lungs. To reduce the chance of being recognized, I'd covered my ash-blond hair with a platinum-blond wig and added two extra layers to my makeup.

"Thank you," I said with an exaggerated sigh as I put the oversized sunglasses back on. "I need a new car, and I'd like to trade in *that*."

A dismissive wave at the front window, outside of which sat a Shelby 427 Cobra. I swore I *heard* jaws drop.

One of the younger salesmen sputtered, "Is that…is that a… It's a replica, right?"

"Certainly not."

"So that's actually a…?"

"An old car," I said. "Yes, yes, I know, it's some kind of collector's piece, but it's old, and I want a new one."

"That's…yours?" an older salesman asked carefully.

"It is now. My granddaddy left it to me. It's very pretty, but"—I scrunched up my nose—"old. It doesn't handle well, and it has no airbags. My parents want me driving something with airbags. So I'm supposed to find a new car. Daddy was going to come with me, but he was called away to Munich last night, and I need something new by the weekend. I have plans."

One of the salesmen stepped forward. The alpha dog, I presumed.

"I can help you, Miss…"

"It's Ms.," I said. "And I'll choose myself, thank you." The mob surged forward, and I let out a throaty laugh. "Down, boys. I need someone experienced and capable. Someone who doesn't think they can treat me like a silly little girl just because I don't know much about cars."

Johnson stood on the fringes, watching with the kind of look that said he knew I'd go for someone younger, hungrier, slicker.

I pointed his way. "You, please."

"Me?"

"Unless you're otherwise occupied…?"

"No, not at all." He walked to me. "Keith Johnson."

THERE'S NO SUBSTITUTE FOR CUBIC INCHES

He smiled. It was a perfectly calm, sincere smile, and in his face, I saw no trace of the man who'd fled ahead of the hounds, who'd demanded to know what he'd done, who'd screamed for mercy.

I shook his hand. "Monica LaSalle." Which was also, coincidentally, the name of the biggest bitch in my debutante class. "Now, I presume you have an office…?"

He led me toward it. "That's a very nice car, Miss—Ms. LaSalle."

"Call me Moni, please. Yes, I know, it's a terrific car, and being perfectly honest, I feel dreadful about trading it in. Granddaddy gave it to me because I loved it so. But I'd never actually driven it, which is an entirely different thing."

He closed the door behind me. "Classic cars are beautiful, but the technology is outdated, both in driving experience and safety."

"Exactly." I tapped his arm and flounced into the chair. "Did you know it doesn't have Bluetooth?"

"I…I imagine it doesn't."

"I understand that they didn't have Bluetooth back then, but I can't even get it retrofitted. So I have to use one of those things that goes over your ear." I shuddered. "Please don't tell my parents, but sometimes, I just use the phone directly while I'm driving, which I know is awfully unsafe."

"It is."

"I've already been pulled over once for it because I was swerving just a tiny bit, but the officer was so sweet. He let me go with a warning."

"I'm sure he did," Johnson mumbled.

I settled into the chair. "Worse, though, I can't connect my playlists. I have to put my phone on the seat and turn the volume all the way up, and the sound quality is just atrocious. Plus, it completely kills my battery, and of course, the car doesn't come with a charging adapter."

"It sounds like you need a new vehicle," he said.

"I do. Daddy wants me to get a Mercedes, but I was driving by your dealership, and I saw that adorable little convertible out front, and I just had to pull in."

"You mean the Audi R8?"

"If that's the black convertible, that's the one. Although, I'd like it in red. Can it come in red?"

"It certainly can. It's an extremely safe vehicle. It has—"

"Is it fast?" I said.

"It's a V10."

I scrunched up my nose.

"That's fast," he said. "And it has Bluetooth with an integrated audio player and a premium sound system."

"Perfect."

"Would you like to take it for a spin?"

"Yes, please. First, though, I need to talk to Daddy. He was very set on a Mercedes, and I would hate to waste your time." I checked my watch. "I should still be able to reach him in Munich. Do you mind?" I waggled my phone.

"Not at all. Let me write down the safety specs for you. Those seem to be very important to your parents, understandably."

As he wrote, I went to turn on my phone.

"No," I breathed. "Oh, damn it. Sorry, I don't mean to curse, but my battery is dead. *Again*." I looked over at his phone. "May I? Don't worry—I'll pay you back for the call."

"No, that's fine. Please go ahead."

He unlocked his phone and pushed it and the specs toward me. I took them. Then I waited. After a moment, he rose.

"Let me give you some privacy," he said.

"Thank you. And please tell me that adorable car has a phone charger?"

He smiled. "It does."

"Perfect."

I took the phone and dialed in a local cell number, randomly. I watched Johnson walk away as the number rang.

"Daddy? It's Moni." I turned my back to the glass door, lowered the phone and set to work as an answering machine connected.

I did quickly check for an outgoing call to the police, but even the most amateur criminal would know better than to use his own phone. Still, there's a lot you can get from a cell once it's been unlocked. Particularly with a USB connector and a handy little black-market device for backing up the data.

"Daddy says no," I said a few minutes later as I walked out and Johnson hurried over. "Which just means I need to talk him into it. It's my car, after all. Things are just easier when Daddy agrees. Can I still get that test drive?"

"Absolutely. Let me go grab the—"

"Oh my God. It's almost five! I am so sorry, Mr. Johnson. This is what happens when my phone dies—I don't get my reminders. I'm supposed to meet my boyfriend for drinks at Eclipse."

When I said that name, he started.

"We don't have reservations," I said as I took out the Cobra's keys. "They are *impossible* to get, but Tucker says if we go for cocktails, we'll get a table—they always reserve a few. Have you ever been there?"

"Eclipse, you said? I haven't heard of it. Popular place, I take it?"

"Crazy popular. Although…" I lowered my voice conspiratorially. "It might not be as busy soon, after what happened to the guy who owns it."

Johnson nodded. He didn't ask what I was talking about. He just nodded.

"Did you hear about that?" I said.

"Uh, no, I didn't. What happened?"

"The owner's wife shot him," I said. "She mistook him for a burglar. Or that's what she told the police, but now I hear she's been arrested."

His head shot up. "Arrested? Do they think it was murder?"

"So they say. I'm not sure if it's in the news yet. I only heard it from my mother. We know the wife's family."

"Yes, of course. Well, that's quite a story."

"It's horrible. I don't believe it myself. I've met Heather, and she's lovely. There's something else going on. I'm sure of it." I reached for his hand. "But I really must go. Thank you again."

I took his hand and squeezed it, and I focused on him, his thoughts, his memories.

Give me a vision. I mentioned Nansen's death. Now show me what Johnson is think—

Darkness.

A car's windshield. Night beyond it. A dark road. Hands gripping a steering wheel. A woman's voice, but he was paying no attention to it. The radio, then.

Johnson gasped. His foot shot out for the brake. Lights. Squealing tires. The car spinning.

The vision stuttered. Johnson's hands again, almost concealed by darkness. One held a cell phone. He lifted the other hand to check his watch. I could see a deflated airbag in the background.

Another stutter.

Johnson was running. I was still inside him, feeling his heart pound, hearing his ragged breath. Behind us, the hounds bayed.

Another stutter.

A newspaper headline. Nansen's death. Johnson's hands gripping the paper as it shook slightly, his breath coming fast.

I snapped from the vision as Johnson dropped my hand. He backed away, blinking hard.

"Are you okay?" I said.

"I…"

"You don't look so good, Mr. Johnson. I think you should sit down."

I put my hand on his arm as I led him to a chair. I hoped for more of the vision, but it was gone. For me to catch a memory-vision, the other person needed to be actively recalling that memory when I made physical contact.

I sat him down. "Let me get you some water."

"No, no. I'm fine. Just a bit dizzy."

"Okay, I'll take off then, but I'm coming back for that test drive. Thank you so much, Mr. Johnson. You've been terrifically kind. I'm sure I'll see you again soon."

SIXTEEN

OLIVIA

I DROPPED off the Cobra at my parents' place, putting it in the garage with the rest of Dad's classic cars.

No, not *Dad's*. Mine. He left these to me, and the only one I'd taken out before now was the Maserati. I'd even been reluctant to use that until my old Jetta mysteriously developed serious engine problems...after Gabriel failed to convince me that if I loved the Maserati, I should drive it.

I don't know what to do with these cars. They deserve to be driven. They deserve to be seen. I supposed Dad envisioned me living the kind of adult life where I'd own an estate like this, with a massive garage like this, and I could do as he had, taking whichever vehicle caught my fancy. I loved these cars, so he bequeathed them to me, and now they sat, gathering dust.

A perfect metaphor for my old life. It sat here, too, the old Olivia, abandoned to rust and rot. Most of my clothes still hung in my closet. My new life held no place for a dozen cocktail dresses or a closet full of shoes. Almost *all* my belongings were still in my room. Treasures that I'd walked away from...and then realized I didn't need.

The house itself had sat empty for the past year, my mother paying for weekly dusting and airing. I didn't know whether she'd ever return or whether, like my former friends, she'd given up on me. The old Liv was gone, and they had no interest in the new one, and I'd be lying if I said that didn't hurt.

I wondered what my father would think of my new life. In my deepest funks, I worried that he would have abandoned me, too, but I knew that was a lie. He'd seen past the old Liv, known there was another one underneath. He'd been the one who'd encouraged me to get my master's. Who'd thought James was a fine young man... but not for me. I didn't think he would actually care about the cars. They were a gift, not an obligation, just like my shares in the department store that bears our family name. I served on the board now, mostly because I felt I should, but I doubted he'd expect that either. I would do it, though, in his memory.

Memory...

That was why I'd come here, besides dropping off the Cobra. Gabriel was busy, and I needed a quiet place to have a conversation with myself. A place to reflect on what I'd gotten from Johnson and untangle that collage of his memories.

I sat by the pool. The sun glistened on the water, and I recalled a recent e-mail from my mother, telling me she'd had the pool opened if I wanted to use it. I would, with Gabriel. It might make the house feel a little less abandoned.

Now I sat on the edge, my boots off, leggings rolled up, legs submerged to mid-calf as I peered into the water, as if it were a scrying glass.

What did I learn from Johnson?

He knew the Nansens. While the evidence was far from conclusive, it was enough for my gut to say, yes. He knew Alan Nansen ran Eclipse, and I suspected he knew Heather came from a wealthy family, given his reaction when I said my family knew hers. *Yes, of course they did.*

If Gabriel were here, he'd point out that I could be misinterpreting the data. Ioan had passed judgment on Johnson for the murder of Alan Nansen. If Johnson remembered the Hunt as a nightmare, might he have not looked up Nansen's name? Learned that Nansen owned Eclipse? Learned that Nansen's wife came from money? And then, in light of that nightmare accusation, deny he knew anything about the crime or the people involved?

Sure…except that I'd skimmed his phone data and found browser history of him reading articles on Nansen's murder *before* the Hunt. He'd been monitoring the case, and he'd known enough to delete that browser history, but not enough to hide his cyber-tracks altogether.

So Johnson was involved. But was that enough to say, yes, the Hunt should take him?

Not yet.

I peered into the water, and I cleared my mind, using some meditative techniques I'd been learning. Focus on the only source of irrefutable data: the vision I'd stolen from Johnson's memory.

Four scenes.

The first, as he was driving the other night, right before he hit Lloergan.

The second, checking his cell phone and watch after the accident set off his airbags. He must have been considering whom he should call, given the hour. A tow truck or a friend or someone from the dealership?

In the third segment, he was running from the Hunt.

The fourth was Johnson reading about Nansen's death in the paper.

The last one didn't add anything new. Nor would I get any fresh information from the Hunt, considering I'd been there. I'd also been present for the accident when Johnson saw Lloergan and—

No.

Well, yes. I'd been there, but this memory was different.

Driving along. A DJ on the radio.

Light.

I'd seen light.

There hadn't been any lights on that empty road, which was why Johnson didn't see Lloergan until the last moment, hitting his brakes just in time to spin out and avoid her.

That was right—he never hit her. But in the vision, his car struck something. A crunch. Then it spun.

The problem with seeing someone else's memories was that we constantly adjust our recollections. If Johnson *thought* he hit another car, could he have reworked his memories to fit? Imagined head-lights? Recalled the crunch of metal on metal?

But he *hadn't* hit Lloergan. His airbags never activated.

So why would Johnson think he'd hit another car?

Something else about the vision wasn't right. I replayed the few seconds of mental video over and over until—

The steering wheel.

A tan steering wheel in a black Audi? Not an impossible color combination, but odd enough that it made me focus on that wheel. On the emblem in the center.

Not an Audi.

Johnson wasn't remembering the incident from the other night. This was a separate accident, somehow spurred by the memory of that Hunt, of Nansen's death.

I grabbed my laptop from my bag.

IT didn't take a PI license to find what I needed. Search for "Keith Johnson" plus "car accident," and the result was…

The reason Johnson was a widower.

He moved to Chicago five years ago, shortly before marrying his wife, Kathy. Three years later, she died. In an automobile accident.

In a hit and run.

An unsolved hit and run.

My mind leapt to a conclusion, but I had to slow down, figure out ways to prove my theory. I had an idea, one that required zooming along a back road of the internet. Trespassing on private cyber-property.

Vehicle licensing and registrations.

And there, I got my lucky break.

Johnson's wife died almost exactly two years ago. The week after that, the Nansens took ownership of a new Land Rover, bought from Alan's dealership-owning brother-in-law. Before that, they'd owned, yep, another Rover. They didn't transfer the license plate, though. They continued paying the license fees and insurance on the old one, which made it look as if they simply bought a second car. No harm in that. But the timing was too coincidental. *Way* too coincidental.

Before I jumped to any conclusions, I placed a call to Heather, who was out on bail.

"Hey, it's Liv Jones. I have a few questions. Can you spare a minute?"

"Of course."

I ran through some questions I'd been accumulating for the defense case. Then, I said, "Okay, now, some of the questions I ask will seem odd, but we're preparing for the prosecution's tactics. They're going to ask why you stayed home after you thought some-one tried to break in those two other nights. They'll try to suggest you weren't too concerned, possibly because no one tried to break in. Gabriel will shut them down, but you'll need to answer their questions if you take the stand. Am I right that you only have one vehicle? That Alan had your car those nights?"

"Yes."

"So you don't own a second vehicle?"

"Right. We only have..." A slight pause, as if she just remem-bered the other Rover. "We *had* two, but we got rid of the second one a while ago."

"Before the break-ins?"

"Yes. Just before that, I think." Another pause. "I never had any reason to drive it, and Alan knew someone who needed a car and couldn't afford it. He gave it to them. He looked after all that, so I don't know the details, but it was definitely gone before the first break-in. I was stuck home alone."

"That's all I needed to know," I said. "Thank you."

SEVENTEEN

GABRIEL

GABRIEL LISTENED as the office door opened and then shut. Heels tapped across it. Not Lydia's sensible pumps or the click of high heels, but the solid thunk that indicated Olivia's boots. He had been waiting nearly thirty minutes, and he was growing impatient, ready to phone and ask where she was.

Olivia would pause to speak to Lydia. On cue, he heard a contralto voice and then Lydia's higher one. Roughly thirty seconds of conversation would ensue, enough for Olivia to greet her and then say, "Is he in?" before crossing to rap at his door. He'd pretend to be busy on his laptop as he said, "I believe I have something on the Johnson case," casual, offhand, as if he had not been drumming his fingers for these thirty minutes, resisting the urge to phone, wanting instead to present it as a gift.

I know how much this case is bothering you, and I wish I could have joined your investigation today, but as soon as I had a free hour, I checked a few things. I have a possible answer, one I know you're looking for. Motive.

He was so caught up in his fantasy revelation that he missed the sound of her boots walking to his door. The next thing he heard was the tap. Except it didn't sound like Olivia's jaunty rap. It sounded...

The door opened, and Lydia peeked in. She held up an envelope, and behind her, he saw a boot-wearing delivery woman walk out.

"Have you heard from Olivia?" Gabriel asked as Lydia handed him the envelope—data for another case.

"If I had, I'd tell you. I know you're waiting."

"I am not—"

She gave him a look that stopped him mid-sentence.

"I have something for her case, so yes, I am waiting."

"You could..." She pointed to his cell phone.

He grumbled under his breath as she withdrew. Then he picked up his phone and sent a text.

Will you be much longer?

She replied in seconds. *Do you need me there?*

Not actually a response to what he asked, but it implied she wasn't exactly on her way, and while he wanted the personal satisfaction of presenting the gift, he shouldn't withhold valuable information.

He called. It connected, the tunnel acoustics telling him she had it on the external Bluetooth in her Maserati.

"We really need to see about getting a connection retrofitted for that," he said, by way of greeting.

"Or I could just get a new car."

"Because your Maserati doesn't come with Bluetooth? That would be ridiculous."

She laughed a little too long, making him feel as if he'd missed a joke.

"So I'm guessing the answer is yes, you need me at the office," she said.

"No, I just had information for you. On the Johnson case. You may wish to investigate the hit-and-run that killed his wife."

He waited for her to ask *what* hit-and-run. When she didn't, he deflated. So much for pulling a rabbit out of a hat.

"You know his wife died in an unsolved hit-and-run, I presume," he said. "That may be a motivation for Johnson. I have the police report here. Johnson said he saw what looked like a small, dark SUV. They were both going around a curve on a paved country road. The other driver lost control. The weather was fine, so it appears to have been careless driving, likely at a high speed. Johnson saw a woman start to get out of the vehicle, but the driver—a man— pulled her back inside, and then they sped off. The descriptions are far from compelling—it was night on a dark road and Johnson had just been hit, his wife in distress. Yet the Nansens did own a black Land Rover, and they purchased a new one a few days later."

Silence. Then, "How long did it take you to get all that?"

"I had a late lunch and ate in."

"So, about an hour. Without leaving your desk." She swore. "I hate you."

"No, I do believe you've said you love me. On multiple occasions. I even have it in writing."

"In writing?"

"Yes, on a note you left me once. I saved it for exactly such an occasion—in case you ever attempt to alter your stance on the matter, I have proof."

She chuckled. "I don't think it works like that."

"Of course it does. Having established that you do not, in fact, hate me, dare I ask what prompted that response?"

"The fact that I've spent all afternoon chasing answers and learned less than you did while eating lunch. Explain to me again why you need an investigator?"

"I don't. But I'm rather fond of you, and you seem to like the job."

Another laugh. "Fair enough. Well, I didn't find out about the hit-and-run until I untangled a vision I got from Johnson. When I brought up Alan Nansen's death, Johnson remembered the Hunt and an accident. Which helps link that accident to Nansen's murder. I learned about the new vehicle through licensing, which they are still paying on the old one, but I also called Heather and spun some bullshit excuse for needing to confirm they only have one car."

"And she did?"

"Yep. But she also quickly mentioned the other one, saying Alan gave it away a while ago, and she knows nothing about that... naturally. My guess is that Alan got his brother-in-law to scrap it. As for the police report of the accident, I was still trying to figure out exactly *where* the accident happened, so I would know which contact to bribe it from. Add all that together, though, and I have no doubt that the Nansens killed Johnson's wife. Alan was driving, and Heather tried to get out and go help, but he stopped her, which I suppose makes Alan more liable, though Johnson still wants revenge against Heather."

"So it seems."

"The problem now is...well, I still don't like it. As Cŵn Annwn justice, I mean. In fact, I'd say it kind of sucks. Technically, Johnson *is* responsible, so I guess it qualifies but..."

"In a court of law, Keith Johnson would have a jury's sympathy, but he would still be charged. This was a meticulously planned revenge."

"And for that, he'd get life?"

"No. Given the circumstances, I would expect a severely reduced sentence. You were hoping he was fully culpable. This is complicated and uncomfortable."

"Putting it mildly," she murmured.

"I'll speak to Ioan."

"Thanks, but this is on me. I have to work this out with him, which will probably mean going on that Hunt and watching… Shit."

"That is unacceptable. Ricky will agree. However much he might trust the Cŵn Annwn, this goes too far. I want to speak to Ioan and confirm that this would be a proper case of Cŵn Annwn justice as it stands now."

"You think there's more to it?"

"I think that, either way, you need that information. I would like to try getting it from him myself. May I do that?"

"All right."

EIGHTEEN

OLIVIA

DID JOHNSON'S case qualify as Cŵn Annwn justice? It was rough justice, to be sure, but absolute justice, too. Ioan had hinted in the past that they didn't consider extenuating circumstances, and I hadn't thought much of it. To me, that term implied excuses. Like using the defense of intoxication. Unless someone poured that booze down your throat, you were still responsible for your actions because you chose to drink, knowing that alcohol impaired judgment.

But what if someone *did* pour it down your throat? Would Cŵn Annwn justice still call you responsible?

I could say it was old-world justice, but was it? I knew enough history to understand the concept of a blood debt. If you killed my wife, I had the right to exact a price, and it might be fifty head of cattle or it might be *your* wife or it might be your *life*. That was the world that gave birth to the Cŵn Annwn.

If Keith Johnson caused Alan Nansen's death for a less righteous reason, I'd accept Ioan's judgment. I didn't care whether Johnson pulled that trigger or not. But if he spurred Heather on as revenge for his wife... I really struggled with the idea that he deserved to have his throat ripped out by a giant hound.

I chose to help both the Tylwyth Teg and the Cŵn Annwn because I believed it was the right thing to do. Divide my power between those who offered fae sanctuary and those who offered fae justice, both equally righteous causes. Yet there was a reason I couldn't choose just one, and it wasn't about righteous causes at all. I made a promise to Ida, the leader of Cainsville, before she died saving me. I promised I would not abandon the Tylwyth Teg. But while Ida saved me, her sacrifice wasn't *for* me—it was about winning me for her town. The Cŵn Annwn had done more for me. They had been honest and fair, so I had to be the same in return.

I had not dug deeper into the ramifications of my promise to the Cŵn Annwn because I feared if I did, I would second-guess my decision, and they did not deserve that. I'd put on my blinders and said, "Sure, I'm okay with hunting killers," and hadn't stopped to consider what exactly that might entail.

Now I had to.

I drove home to Cainsville and walked to the diner. A man sat at the corner table, windows on two sides, the best seat in the house. Not that he noticed—his gaze was glued to his laptop screen as his fingers flew over the keys. He looked about my age, sharp-featured, dark hair to his shoulders, goatee, dressed in jeans and boots, needing only a man-bun to complete the look of a café poet, laboring on his latest ode to cold-brewed coffee.

I picked up the coffee pot from the serving station. It was the regular stuff—no cold-brew here, where you'll get a scowl if you ask for decaf. The owner—Larry—smiled and said nothing as I took the pot. I walked up behind Patrick and, without looking from his keyboard, he lifted his mug.

"My favorite server returns," he said.

I filled his mug, returned the pot and slid into the seat across from him. "I need access to your books."

"Lovely to see you, too, Liv. How are you? And how is my son? I haven't seen him around in a few days."

"I filled your coffee, bòcan, which buys me a ticket past the small talk."

Patrick lifted a brow. "No, I believe the coffee buys you access to that seat. Small talk is still required, to make me feel like a valuable ally rather than your personal librarian."

"All right. I'm not fine, at the moment. That's why I'm here to see you. Gabriel is doing well enough, considering he has to endure visits with his mother, which I'm trying to curb. Is that what you wanted? Or would you rather I just said we're both doing awesome?"

"We need to talk about the Seanna issue. I'm glad you brought that up. But first, let's deal with your problem. We can discuss it on the way." He closed his laptop.

"How's the writing going?" I asked.

He smiled. "Thank you. I'll even pretend you care and aren't just tossing me a bone. I've hit a point in the novel where I know where I'm heading but am not quite sure how to get there, so a break is a very welcome distraction."

"Meaning you now owe *me?* Cool."

"That depends on your request. To be distracting, it must also be interesting. Otherwise, you still owe me."

❧

"NOW that is how you commit a murder," Patrick said as I finished telling him the story. "Ingenious."

"On paper, yes. In reality, he just got lucky. Johnson, that is. Not Alan...or Heather."

"Oh, I think the jury is still out on Heather. Both literally—depending on the outcome of the charges—and figuratively. The loss of a spouse doesn't always affect one quite as dramatically as it did poor Mr. Johnson. But it's a brilliant plot that could either succeed or go horribly awry. Both are equally good fodder for fiction."

I turned onto his street. "Mmm, pretty sure there's a third—and far more likely—option there. That the plan goes nowhere at all. Johnson set up the board, but Heather had to make the final play, and all it would have taken was for Alan to say 'Honey, I'm home!' and he'd still be alive."

"Unless..." He waved it off. "I'll save *that* for a book plot. So yes, I do owe you for this one."

"Great. But I'm not actually here to entertain you. There's a moral to this story. A moral quandary."

"There is, isn't there? A delicious ethical conundrum."

"Far less delicious when you're the one experiencing it."

"Oh, I wouldn't know." He took out his house keys. "But the way I see it, Mr. Johnson took this chance knowingly. He rolled the dice. He realized that the end result, no matter how clever he'd been, could be his arrest and subsequent jail time."

"And execution? I don't think he was counting on that."

"No one ever counts on death by cŵn. Which is a shame. People might be far more respectful of fae if they knew the punishment for harming us."

"Which would first require them to know about fae."

"And that would be terribly inconvenient. As for Mr. Johnson, I'll argue that when one commits murder in revenge, one must

accept the possibility of counter-revenge. An eye for an eye seems all well and good until everyone's blind."

"True," I said as I climbed his steps.

"I would also argue that Mr. Nansen, while an entitled ass, did not intend to kill Mrs. Johnson. So is killing *him* justifiable? If you were to take a corner too fast in your little sports car, hit another vehicle, panic and flee, would you deserve to die for the crime? No court of law would say yes. No more than it would agree to kill Mr. Johnson for *his* crime."

He pushed open the door. "If you don't get the answers you want from my books, Liv, that might be what you need to remember."

"Two wrongs don't make a right."

"So I've heard."

"Thank you."

He glanced back at me, brows raised.

"I mean it," I said. "Thank you for that rationale. I have a feeling I might need it."

NINETEEN

OLIVIA

ONE WOULD expect a writer to have books, of course, but Patrick's were unique. Not the ones he wrote—those were currently paranormal romance. I mean the reference books on his shelf. He might snark about me treating him like my personal librarian, but he was indeed the local archivist, even if he held the title unofficially. He collected books written by fae, and they were...a unique reading experience.

Patrick walked to one shelf and took down a book on the Cŵn Annwn. Ioan didn't know Patrick had it. If he did, he might demand it back. The Cŵn Annwn were *not* archivists—they were more book-burners, sometimes literally. Chronicling real tales of fae or Hunt life was dangerous, risking exposure, so the Cŵn Annwn preferred an oral tradition.

The book Patrick handed me was one I'd read before, by a Huntsman whose views fell more in line with Patrick's own on the value of historical record. He'd written a massive tome on everything he knew about Cŵn Annwn history. After his death, his fellow Huntsmen hadn't known quite what to do with the book. Pages were burned, as if it'd been thrown into a fire but then yanked out again. Some pages were torn away. Others had passages redacted with heavy ink.

The book made the Cŵn Annwn nervous, but they couldn't bring themselves to destroy their brother's work completely. If they'd known it would end up in the hands of a Tylwyth Teg elder, they might have tried a little harder.

I skimmed the pages, mentally translating the Welsh. I tipped my hat to the Huntsman who wrote it, and I was sure Patrick did too. The man wasn't just some amateur, jotting down notes as they came to him. The book was meticulously organized by section, and I only had to flip through until I came to the part I wanted. Justice.

I'd read enough of this book to confirm that everything Ioan had told me about the Cŵn Annwn was true. I expected no less. For a branch of fae, the Cŵn Annwn were astonishingly resistant to lying. Perhaps not so astonishing, I guess, if they'd broken from the main group and established themselves as a separate entity with a clear mission and a very different worldview.

I trusted Ioan to be honest with me. The problem was that, being from an oral tradition, he was largely reliant on his own experience and that of his predecessors. If they hadn't experienced a thing, they knew little about it.

The Huntsman author began the justice section with explanations. All things I knew. Cŵn Annwn hunted humans who killed fae or fae-blood humans. It wasn't like a bat signal that went off every time one died. Instead, the Cŵn Annwn became aware of their prey in different ways. For example, I'd seen visions of Cŵn Annwn ravens circling the site of an ancient massacre, looking for fae-blood humans among the dead. I'd also had visions of Huntsmen walking past a human, looking at his eyes and getting an inner alert that said: *this one.* In the case of fae deaths, the news also traveled through the fae, and the Cŵn Annwn would investigate. All this meant that not everyone who deserved a Cŵn Annwn death got one—just the killers they came across, one way or another.

Once the Cŵn Annwn had their prey, they tracked him or her, using their ravens and hounds. They needed to get their quarry to a forest for the actual Hunt. That was the only way they could take a life.

But the author did more than just expatiate. He gave examples. That was the part I needed. I learned best when shown. And Patrick's books really did show me.

I ran my finger over the text, and the writing began to blur and pulse, and then the words opened up, and I fell through into darkness, smelling damp forest, a cold spring chill in the air.

I heard a voice then. As always, while I doubted I was listening to modern English, that was what I heard. "Albert Mays, you have been found guilty in the murder of your wife and her lover."

The scene cleared, and I saw a medieval peasant held in the jaws of a cŵn, the pack around their alpha, a mounted Huntsman towering over them.

"Your life is forfeit for theirs," the Huntsman said, voice booming from inside his cowl.

"Wh-what? No. The law set me free. Within my rights, they said, walking in on them like that. They had it coming, they did."

"No, they did not. Your wife broke her marriage vow. That is a violation of contract. Nothing more. The human courts might set you free, but we do not. Now run!"

The scene darkened again as I tumbled into another vision, this time hitting the ground in a bog, the stink of death and decay heavy in the air. A woman crouched by a well-trodden path through the swamp. She wore even older garb, from the time of nomadic Celtic clans. Night had just begun to fall. A dog howled in the distance, and she listened. Then she shook her head and settled back into her crouch.

"Are you sure you wish to hear the hounds?" a man's voice asked.

The woman leapt up, drawing a blade from under her cloak. "Who's there?"

"A concerned passerby." A man stepped out. He was about my age, with a thick fur over his shoulders and a bow across his shoulder. He lifted his hands. "I am unarmed."

She snorted. "A man doesn't need arms to be a threat to a woman."

"True enough." He stopped a few feet away. "Is this better?"

A rustle sounded in the bushes, and she spun. The man gave a low whistle and waved his arm.

"Merely my hound," he said. "I've sent him off."

She peered at him. "I don't know you."

"Do you know everyone in these woods?"

"Yes."

He smiled. "Perhaps not, then, if you don't know me. You might not wish to pursue your current course."

"And what might that be?"

"Waiting for the Cŵn Annwn. Do you think the Huntsmen enjoy finding humans lying in wait for them? They have business to attend to, and they do not appreciate the distraction from their Hunt."

"I have business with *them*. My husband has been murdered, and his family say they have the blood of the fair folk in their veins."

"Hmm." The man eyed the woman, his gaze piercing hers. "Killed in war?"

"Yes, with a neighboring clan."

"And he was a warrior, taken down in the field by yet another warrior?"

"Yes. Murdered—"

"No, killed in battle. Having willingly *gone* to battle. Slain fairly. That is not the concern of the Hunt."

She bristled. "He had fae blood—"

"Perhaps, but it would not matter."

"That is for the Cŵn Annwn to decide."

"I would suggest that they already have."

Another rustle, and the woman turned as a giant black hound stepped out. She staggered back. The man raised his hand, stopping the cŵn. Then he turned to the woman.

"You will go home, yes?" he said.

She nodded.

"Good. Mourn your husband there and hope that your children's generation will not find war-making quite so palatable a solution to their disputes."

After that vision had faded, I tumbled through two more, one from the eighties, a woman in big hair and aviator frames fleeing from the Hunt, swearing she'd killed her lover in a drug-induced rage. The lead Huntsman said it did not matter—she took the drugs of her own free will, and thus she was guilty.

The other vignette was set in the thirties or forties, with a man calling on the Hunt to avenge the death of his brother, strangled by a friend during a psychotic break. Like the woman in the swamp, his case was refused. The young man had sought help for his illness and been ignored; therefore, the death was not his fault, but that of the society that turned its back on him.

When I surfaced from the visions, I sat there a moment, assimilating.

Then Patrick said, "And..."

"I saw four cases. Four instances where the Cŵn Annwn decided whether or not a death deserved punishment. Crime of passion? Yes.

A cheating spouse doesn't justify murder. Killed in battle? No. You signed up for that. Acted under the influence? Yes. Again, you took that chance. Mental illness, after having sought help? No, you tried to prevent actions that *are* beyond your control."

"Reasonable."

"Exactly. I agree with the Cŵn Annwn in every one of those cases. Which all suggest I'm missing something in my solution to Alan Nansen's death."

I rose. "Thanks for the library access. I should get going. If Gabriel doesn't need me back at the office, I might actually surprise him by making dinner while I think this through."

"Speaking of my son, you mentioned issues with his visits to Seanna. Shocking, really. No one could ever foresee how *that* would go wrong. Oh, wait. I believe I did. Note, for the record, then, please, that I objected, both to the visits and to keeping you out of the loop."

I hesitated, my purse in hand. Then I rolled my eyes. "Yep, keeping things from me is never a good idea, which you'd think Gabriel would know by now."

"Well, I'm glad he came clean, and since you don't seem terribly upset, I appreciate that you understood his motivation."

"I'm trying."

He got to his feet. "I know I was ready to let Pamela kill Seanna..."

"Let her? Pretty sure you were *facilitating* it. After I asked you to *stop* her."

"A misunderstanding. But I will admit now that you were right. If Gabriel had stood by and let that happen, while he might tell himself he didn't care, he would have suffered guilt that he doesn't deserve. So whatever is happening now, it's not your fault."

"Good to know."

"How's Rose handling Gabriel not going anymore?"

"I haven't spoken to her yet, so I'd rather you didn't mention it."

"Oh, I won't. And…" He lowered his voice. "Don't be angry with our Rose. If she had any idea those visits bothered Gabriel, she'd have stopped calling him. But you know how he is."

"I know exactly how he is."

I thanked Patrick for his help—all of it—and then left.

Apparently, I needed to pay a visit to Rose.

TWENTY

GABRIEL

GABRIEL STEPPED off the elevator just as one of the Huntsmen was getting on.

"Gw—Gabriel." The Huntsman pumped Gabriel's hand. "Good to meet you. I don't think we've been officially introduced. I'm Aeron, though around here it's Aaron." He turned to lead Gabriel into a suite of upscale offices. "Were you looking for Ioan?"

"I was, thank you."

Gabriel hadn't been here before—this was a part of Olivia's life that he left to Ricky. Unlike the fae—who usually lived off ill-gotten gains—the Cŵn Annwn ran a business. Gwylio Consulting, a security firm.

Aeron wore a suit nearly as expensive as Gabriel's own, as did the other men they passed, all Huntsmen, looking no different than any successful businessman one might find in the Loop. The only women were support staff—humans, all of them, with no idea that they worked for anyone who wasn't.

Aeron waved to Ioan's assistant, walked to an office door and rapped. Then he poked his head in with, "Gabriel Walsh to see you, John."

Ioan said something, and Aeron pushed open the door. Gabriel walked through, and as the door closed behind him, the already hushed sounds of the office disappeared. Excellent soundproofing allowing the Cŵn Annwn to speak freely within their offices.

"Gabriel," Ioan said, walking from behind his desk, hand extended.

It took Gabriel a split second to offer his hand. No ill-will intended—he simply wasn't accustomed to such a greeting from the Cŵn Annwn leader. It was a byproduct of the environment. That was how the Huntsmen had adapted and assimilated to human life. When in a business setting, one acts and reacts in a business-like way.

They shook hands, and Ioan gestured to a chair and then offered a hot or cold beverage, which Gabriel refused.

"I'm here on Olivia's behalf," he said as he sat.

"I presumed as much." Ioan smiled. "I doubted you were seeking a security contract. When you say you're here on her behalf, may I hope that only means you're helping her investigate? I'm sure you aren't happy with what happened the other night..."

"I would not come here to complain," Gabriel said, his tone cooling. "Olivia hardly needs me to fight her battles."

Ioan frowned. "Do you see this as a battle, Gabriel? The Cŵn Annwn as something Liv has to fight?"

"I hope not."

"We aren't. I know this first Hunt was a rough one, and I could say I'd rather she had an easy one her first time, but I'd be lying. Difficult is good. It lays all the cards on the table. Lets her see exactly what she's getting into and gives her the chance to deal with that."

"So you're admitting you knew this Hunt had complications?"

A moment of silence, as if the Cŵn Annwn leader may have let on more than he intended.

"*That* I do not appreciate," Gabriel said. "You have positioned yourself as the more honest alternative to the fae. The more forthright. The less manipulative."

"I didn't lie to her or manipulate—"

"You allowed her to begin a Hunt you knew she might not be able to finish…and then suffer the embarrassment of derailing it."

"I…" Ioan rubbed his mouth. "I didn't realize it would be embarrassing for her. I saw that at the time, and I apologize. To both of you."

Gabriel eased back. "As I said, I didn't come here to complain or berate you. I wished to update you on her progress. On what she has discovered about Keith Johnson's possible involvement."

Ioan waved his hand. "That isn't necessary. The investigation is for Liv. To reassure her that Johnson is guilty."

"And you know he is."

"Yes."

"Based on a power that has never been found to be faulty."

Ioan met his gaze. "Yes. I can say, with absolute confidence, that we have never taken our quarry and found it to be a mistake."

"That would be far more reassuring if you took any interest in the actual circumstances, investigated beforehand or followed up afterward to be sure."

Ioan's cheek twitched. "I know you are a lawyer, and your job is to poke holes in my testimony, but there is a reason the Cŵn Annwn do not investigate, and it isn't laziness. It isn't blind faith, nor is it fear of discovering something that might make us reconsider. It's efficiency, Gabriel, and I have a feeling you understand that concept very well. We know our target is guilty, so why would we waste time investigating? As for follow-up, we actually do some of that, to be sure no innocent party is later accused of the crime. That has happened. In that case, we help the falsely accused by providing evidence—true evidence—that sends the police in the correct direction. Never, in any of those instances, has anyone else been found guilty of a crime for which we executed another person."

"Then I would like you to listen to the details of this case and explain Olivia's findings."

Gabriel told Ioan about the murder, Heather's arrest, and the death of Johnson's wife, along with the evidence strongly suggesting the Nansens were responsible.

"That..." Ioan leaned back in his chair, his brow furrowed. "That does not... That isn't correct."

"If you have evidence to contradict Olivia's findings—"

"I mean that it doesn't fit the criteria."

"Which part?"

Ioan threw up his hands. "Any of it. We may not investigate our quarry, but we often see—through visions—the details of the crime. Or we uncover those details in our postmortem. Or we simply hear about them as humans do—on the news, in passing, in conversation."

"And this case differs from those *how* exactly?"

"Not every case is clear cut. There are those where a jury would allow for extenuating circumstances... Yes, I'll be honest, we find human laws less conservative than our own. There are so many"—his hands fluttered—"excuses."

"The Cŵn Annwn do not accept excuses."

"Explanations, yes. Excuses, no. There is a difference, as I'm sure you'll recognize."

"I'm a defense attorney. I prefer *not* to recognize the distinction. It's bad for business."

Ioan let out a laugh. "I'm sure it is. But you personally recognize it. I know you do. The Cŵn Annwn may set the line in a different place, but we're certainly not going to do something like hunt down a woman who killed her abusive husband in self-defense. In cases like that, I daresay we're even more liberal than your courts."

"And in a case where a man sought revenge on his wife's killers?"

"I'll admit, this is a gray area. If Johnson knew for certain that they had intentionally murdered her, then no, he would not be a target. As it stands... I can only say that we've never encountered a case like this. Add that to the fact that he didn't actually commit the murder..."

"That too is unusual?"

"Again, I can't think of an instance of that. It's possible, of course. If a human paid money to murder a fae, then clearly that person could not escape our justice simply because he didn't pull the trigger. That, I believe, is similar to human law."

"It is."

"Many years ago, a case was brought to our attention by a full-blood fae whose mate had worked for a man in organized crime. She had attempted to blackmail her employer. He had complained to an underling about it, saying she was a problem he'd pay dearly to solve."

"Will no one rid me of this turbulent priest?"

Ioan smiled. "Yes, and while we can trace the murder of Thomas Becket back to Henry the Second, it isn't quite the same as telling one of his men to murder the archbishop. When I was asked by this fae to avenge his mate, I went to see her former employer. I looked him in the eye, and whatever internal scale we possess, it did not tip against him. He was not culpable enough. The man who actually killed her, though? Yes. He was guilty. The *initiative* remained his. The decision was his. Not the employer's."

"What you are suggesting, then, is that there is more to Johnson's story."

"Yes, I believe so."

TWENTY-ONE

OLIVIA

A CAR parked in front of Rose's house told me she had a client. I headed across the road to where Grace perched on her front stoop.

"How's Seanna today?" I asked.

"Quiet."

"As usual?"

Grace looked up at me, her sunken eyes narrowing. Then she said, "No."

"Not as usual?"

"I mean, no, I'm not falling for this."

"Falling for what? I asked a simple question."

She snorted. "And I am not a *simpleton*. You think I don't see that look in your eye? I had only to watch you march up that street to know you are a girl with a mission. First to Rose, who's busy. Then you spot me and change course like a guided missile sighting a new target. I know what you're here for, and I know you just came from Patrick's. That fool bòcan might slip and tell you something he shouldn't. I will not."

"But you know what I'm asking about, don't you?"

"You already said it."

I met her gaze. "And so did you. You said Seanna's quiet today, which implies she isn't always, yet as far as I know, she's an absolute lamb. Poor, addled Seanna is no trouble at all."

"It has nothing to do with me."

"Seanna's less-than-quiet moments? Or the cover-up?"

She looked me in the eye. "Both."

"Thank you," I said, and headed back across the road.

I let myself into Rose's house. She had her client in the parlor. I could hear Rose reading the cards, telling the client that she faced a decision, one that would decide the path of her future.

As I tiptoed past, I peeked in and motioned to Rose that I'd be in the kitchen. Then I closed the parlor door. Ten minutes later, I was taking the tea bags out of the pot when the front door shut. A moment later, the kitchen doorway darkened.

"I need to talk to you," I said.

"I guessed that much. I don't suppose you're looking for a reading."

I lifted the tea tray as I turned to face her. "I don't know. Can the cards help me figure out why the people I trust most in this town conspired to keep me from knowing about Seanna?"

Her cheek twitched. "Gabriel told you."

"Ha. No. That would be too easy. I had this really weird delusion that after we got together, he'd stop lying to me, stop keeping things from me, but that's just me being naive. If a guy is one thing before you start a relationship, don't expect that to change afterward. I knew better. I just hoped, you know?"

I walked past her into the parlor.

"He didn't want to upset you," she said as she followed me.

"Yeah, because I love being coddled." I set the tray down with a clack.

"He doesn't do that, Liv."

I turned to her. "I didn't come to discuss Gabriel's motives. I came to discuss yours."

"Mine?"

"First, just so there isn't any confusion, no one *tattled*. I was speaking to Patrick, and I mentioned, off-hand, that Gabriel was struggling with his visits to Seanna, and I've convinced him to take a break from them. I meant the times Gabriel and I visit Seanna for tea. Patrick thought I meant the other times—the ones I didn't know about. An innocent mistake. But Patrick did make it clear he really wasn't happy about the situation. So did Grace. In other words, I get the feeling that both of them thought Gabriel should tell me. If you had also counseled him to tell me, that would have been the tipping point. But he didn't. Therefore, *you* didn't."

Her blue eyes frosted.

Before she could speak, I said, "Yes, I'm crossing a line. Family business. None of mine. But you and Patrick both tell me how good I am for Gabriel. How much he needs someone who supports him unconditionally. Who watches out for his best interests. Yet if watching out for those interests means crossing a line with you or Patrick? That's when I get my hand slapped."

"I'm not slapping your hand, Liv. I just don't like the way you seem to be suggesting that I *don't* have his best interests at heart."

"Oh, but you do. Can I be totally presumptuous here and hazard a guess at your motive?"

She reached for the teapot, her voice still cool as she said, "Please do."

"You want reconciliation between Seanna and Gabriel. Or maybe reconciliation is too strong a word. You want Seanna to find peace, to be as happy as she can be in her present state. And you want Gabriel to find peace, too. To come to see another side of Seanna, one he never got to see as a child."

Rose didn't answer for a moment. Then she said, "You say he's upset. I think you're mistaken. You expect him to be upset, so you see it. I don't."

I nodded. "Okay. Sure, I'm the one who *lives* with him, but maybe I'm wrong. Maybe when I suggested he stop our tea visits, he only agreed because he's busy."

Her mouth opened.

I kept going. "I know he's taking off at night. I'm guessing he's going to deal with Seanna. Grace hinted that Seanna isn't always as quiet as when I see her. So something happens, she wakes up agitated, and Gabriel goes to help you calm her, and he's not telling me because he knows I'll worry that I've supported the wrong course of action with Seanna, that in balancing your needs and his, I weighed too heavily in your favor."

She pulled back. Took a cookie. Broke off a piece and then stared at it before putting it, uneaten, onto her saucer.

"Yes, she wakes upset," Rose said. "Very upset and calling for Gabriel."

I tensed. "*Calling* for him?"

"He's the only one she wants. The only one who can calm her down."

"So he's not going as additional help. He's going because he has to."

Her mouth tightened. "I've told him he doesn't need to—"

"And make you handle her tantrums? Never. If you need him, he's there. What happens after he shows up?"

"They talk. She acts like a mother. In those moments, she actually behaves like Gabriel's mother."

Which was what Rose wanted to see. Desperately.

"For example…?" I prodded.

"She asks him about work. She brings up things from their past. Memories. Good ones."

I bit my tongue against saying there were no good ones.

"Such as…?" I prodded again.

"The playground. She mentioned that she remembered taking him to playgrounds."

My gut went cold. Rose kept talking, something about suspecting Seanna hadn't been there pushing him on the swings, but this showed that she'd been trying.

"Trying," I said, barely able to get the word out. "It showed she'd been…trying."

I met her gaze. "Seanna used to lock Gabriel in a cubby hole while she whored. Once, she left him there for days. When she tried to put him back in after that, he panicked. So she started dropping him off at the playground. For hours. Sometimes all night, because you know, it'd just be inconvenient to get out of bed after the guy leaves and have to go pick up your four-year-old son at the playground. Your *four-year-old son*."

When I saw Rose's expression, I wanted to suck the words back in. Instead, I sat there, my heart slamming, the voice in my head screaming that I'd fucked up, screwed up, betrayed a trust, hurt someone who did not deserve to be hurt.

"I… I…" Rose said. "I didn't—"

I pushed the chair back and scrambled up. "I'm sorry. I'm so sorry. I shouldn't have—"

"No," she said, rising. "You should have. If that is what Seanna was doing, I needed to know."

I shook my head and paced across the room. "Gabriel wouldn't want you to. He *never* wanted you to know how bad it got, back then, and he doesn't want you to know now. He knows you...you feel guilty over not doing more, but you tried—he understands that, and you never realized how bad it was, because that was his choice. It's still his choice and—" I pressed my palms to my eyelids. "And now I've..."

Hot tears filled my eyes. "God, that was stupid. I'm sorry. To both of you, I'm really, really—"

Her arms went around me in an awkward embrace. "If Gabriel doesn't want me to know, then there's no reason he needs to know that I do."

I pulled back and looked at her with a twisted smile. "Isn't that how we get in these situations? Keeping secrets for someone's own good?" I exhaled. "No, I have to tell him. It's uncomfortable, and he doesn't want to be that person. It makes him feel like a victim. I tell him he's a survivor, not a victim."

She squeezed my arm. "I know you didn't mean to tell me, Liv, but I'm glad you did. This was another one of those secrets—we keep it to protect someone, and it just makes everything so much worse. If I had any idea—*any*—" Her breath caught. "I would never have agreed to have Seanna stay in Cainsville."

"But I did know, and I still supported her staying."

"For me. Because I wanted it, and you thought you could protect Gabriel from her, and I..." She nodded. "You're right. I wanted some form of reconciliation."

"I think that's possible," I said carefully, "maybe even necessary—for him—but not like this. He needs to be in a situation where no one gives a damn whether he chooses to see Seanna or not. Where it is entirely up to him. Where he doesn't feel he's pleasing—or displeasing—either of us by doing it. No guilt. No pressure. No judgment."

She nodded. "Yes. That's what I wanted, but it wouldn't matter how often I told him that I didn't care whether he came—he knew I did. I realized he might be uncomfortable. I just… I thought it was best. For her, yes, but mostly for him."

"The temporary discomfort of a scab before healing."

"Yes. But with her bringing up the playground and other memories, he was more than uncomfortable. He must have been."

"He hides it well." As I moved back to my chair, I said, "Is there any chance—?" Then I cut myself off with a shake of my head.

"What?"

I hesitated before saying, carefully, "It's entirely possible that Seanna only remembers taking him to playgrounds and presumes it was a good memory for him."

"But is there any chance she knows better?"

"Yes."

Rose was silent for a minute, and I was about to move on, just let the possibility sit there, no need to pursue it. Then she said, "I don't know, Liv. I want to say no, that given her demeanor, it seems only that she recalls a playground, and there's no chance she could be tormenting—"

She inhaled sharply. "What you've told me says that things in their life together were even worse than I imagined. In light of that, I don't even know how to interpret her behavior. She insists on seeing him. She's very affectionate. She brings up memories. It could be exactly what I hoped—that she's forgotten the worst and is finally acting like a mother, but... I don't know. We need more time to assess this."

"More time *without* Gabriel around her."

"Definitely."

TWENTY-TWO

OLIVIA

AFTER LEAVING Rose, I drove back to the city, and I thought. I thought a lot. Then I made a couple of stops and a phone call before heading to the office.

"Any sign of the boss?" I asked as I walked in.

No one answered. I looked at Lydia's empty desk and checked my watch. It was past six. I sent off a text to Gabriel, telling him where he could find me, and went into his office to work.

When I started at the firm, Gabriel assigned me the meeting room as an office—there wasn't a separate room for me to work in. Most times, though, he had preferred me in his office where he didn't have to get up to talk to me. When he got around to buying a second desk, he'd just had them put it in his office, and that was where I stayed.

Today, though, I sat at the big desk. His desk. I riffled through the stack of files on it until I found the police report from the accident that killed Johnson's wife.

Something wasn't fitting with the scenario I'd worked out— Alan Nansen killed Kathy Johnson in a hit-and-run, and then two years later, her husband initiated an elaborate scheme to get Heather to kill Alan.

Time to go back to the beginning of that solution and reanalyze the data. According to the report, it played out as I'd seen in the vision. Dark country road. Johnson was driving. His wife was in the passenger seat. It would have been her voice I heard, Johnson paying no attention to what she was saying. According to the report, they'd reached a curve, and the next thing Johnson knew, he saw a flash of headlights...and then impact.

The collision happened too fast for Johnson to even process what happened. Their car spun off the road and down an embankment. It struck a tree on the passenger side. Johnson had groggily looked around and spotted another vehicle with a woman climbing out, only to be pulled back inside. Johnson lost consciousness before he really understood what he was seeing.

When he woke up, he immediately checked on his wife. She wasn't breathing. He frantically dialed 911. Paramedics arrived within twenty minutes, but it was too late. His wife was dead.

The police had tried to find the person responsible. They tried even harder than usual, I suspected, not only because there was a death involved, but because, if someone in the other car had called 911, Kathy Johnson would still be alive. It was the delay that killed her. The car went off the road in a quiet area, and it spun down into an embankment at night, where any cars that passed continued by, oblivious.

I could now see why Johnson would definitely blame Alan Nansen. A hit-and-run causing death was bad enough. But in fleeing the scene, the Nansens *let* Kathy Johnson die. Even an anonymous 911 call from a pay phone would have saved her.

That scenario, however, made Johnson seem *less* accountable for Alan's death, which took it even farther out of the Cŵn Annwn's realm.

I glanced at my silent cell phone. I really could use Gabriel's help on this. I needed someone to bounce ideas off, someone to see what I must be missing. But he wasn't returning my text, meaning he was busy, and I hated to interrupt for something that wasn't urgent. We could discuss it over dinner.

Thinking of dinner, I checked my watch. And then I stopped. I stared at my watch. Looked at my cell phone. Back at my watch.

I remembered Johnson's memories. A flash of a cell phone in his hand, his gaze going to it and then to his watch. I'd thought that was after the accident with Lloergan, but his airbags hadn't gone off then. So this was connected to his wife's accident.

Why had he remembered that exact moment?

Because that was when he'd realized it was too late. He'd regained consciousness and looked at his watch...

Somehow, even addle-brained, I couldn't imagine I'd wake up after an accident, see Gabriel unconscious and check my watch. If by some bizarre chance "Hey, how long have I been out?" was the next thing on my mind, I'd glance at the time *while* calling 911.

There had to be a reason why he'd remembered that moment, along with the accident and the Hunt and seeing the headline of Nansen's death. A connection that I wasn't making...

I pictured his watch again.

Oh, yes. Oh, *hell* yes.

I grabbed the report.

Johnson told the police he didn't know exactly when they'd gone off the road. They'd left the city just past midnight, but he hadn't checked the time since. The police knew, though. They got that data from the car's computer to help in their investigation.

The accident happened at 12:32 a.m. Johnson placed the 911 call at 1:59 a.m. And the time on his watch when he glanced at it?

Just past one in the morning.

I leafed through the pages for the paramedics' report. They arrived and immediately went to Kathy Johnson's aid. Once they'd determined they couldn't revive her, they wanted to check out Johnson's condition, but he was agitated and distraught and insisted on getting his wife to a hospital. He could be checked there if necessary, but he'd only suffered a crack on the head. Once at the hospital, he'd refused treatment.

Because you didn't crack your head, did you, Keith?

What would you crack it on? The airbags deployed. Your wife died from the impact of the tree on the passenger's side. You were cushioned by the airbags.

You were fine.

If Keith Johnson did pass out, it was only briefly. He'd been awake and alert just after one, midway between the time of the accident and calling 911. He'd checked his watch because he was waiting.

Waiting until it was too late to save her.

Keith Johnson killed his wife. It didn't matter if he hadn't caused the accident. He'd taken advantage of it, and that was even more coldhearted than what the Nansens did. He sat in that car and waited for his wife to die.

And then he went after the Nansens?

That didn't make any sense. Especially not if he waited two years to do it.

The only reason he would target the Nansens was if they were in danger of being arrested. That would reopen the case, and the lawyers would be all over it, analyzing details in a way the police hadn't needed to. But I saw absolutely no suggestion that the police had reopened the investigation.

What happened, Keith?

I turned my attention to his phone data and began excavating. Phone calls. Texts. Calendar appointments. E-mails.

And that's where I found it. A deleted e-mail, dated two weeks before the first break-in attempt, sent to Johnson from an anonymous account.

I sent a quick text to Gabriel and took off.

TWENTY-THREE

GABRIEL

ON LEAVING Gwylio Consulting, Gabriel pulled out his phone. He'd left Olivia a message earlier, and she'd texted back, saying she'd been at Patrick's, using his books. Her research confirmed Ioan's claims—there was no evidence the solution they'd uncovered *should* warrant Cŵn Annwn justice. But Gabriel was still certain they were on the right track. They were merely missing elements.

Gabriel had wanted to talk about that, but Olivia had been racing off in pursuit of another angle. Disappointing, yes, but it did give him the chance to do what he'd failed to manage earlier: surprise her with new data.

Before Olivia, Gabriel had acted as investigator for all his own cases. He'd considered contracting one for the more mundane work, such as surveilling witnesses, but that would have meant giving an outsider access to his defense strategy, and while other attorneys did so, his personal methods made that more complicated.

As for the not-so-mundane points of investigation, he'd never considered relinquishing those. He told himself it was even riskier to contract those out, but the truth was that he liked that part. He liked digging for clues, following the trail, solving the mystery. Only one thing proved better than investigating by himself—investigating with Olivia.

Ioan's office was close to Gabriel's condo, so he went there to think in peace and find that new data.

Ioan didn't like their solution. And there was one part that Olivia hadn't liked either, initially.

Heather Nansen.

As a defense lawyer, Gabriel knew there were many ways one could react to the death of a loved one. He could attribute Heather's reaction to shock. Yet given the fact that she was responsible for her husband's death, even Gabriel had expected a stronger response.

Their solution to the crime exonerated Heather Nansen as much as she could ever be exonerated. That is, it said that Keith Johnson had deliberately staged the break-ins in hopes of driving Heather to shoot her husband. Her guilt, then, was only that of a person who made a fatal and tragic mistake.

Or was it?

What if this case had been presented to Gabriel without the Cŵn Annwn claiming another person was responsible? What if he removed Johnson from the equation?

He would have thought Heather guilty. Her story was simply too odd. Gabriel and Olivia had acknowledged that—repeatedly— yet knowing that Ioan blamed Johnson, those oddities had only seemed proof that a third party was indeed involved.

But if Gabriel removed Johnson from the game board, he would never have accepted the case. It contained far too many weak points.

Someone broke into our house. And then tried twice more, and no, he didn't succeed, but I was so terribly worried that I bought a gun.

You think I lured my husband home? Gracious, no. Didn't I tell you someone stole my phone? That person must have sent the texts.

Heather had believed that herself until Olivia corrected her, which showed a poor understanding of technology. Gabriel himself had a better one, but it still wasn't his forte. For that, he *did* reach out and get external expertise.

Gabriel placed a call to Lydia's grandson, a nineteen-year-old student at Caltech, who had absolutely no interest in the defense strategy of some Chicago lawyer, but a very vested interest in his bank account, which grew whenever he received phone calls from said lawyer.

"It's Gabriel Walsh," he said when Bryant answered.

"You do know that your name appears on the little screen when you call, right, Gabriel?" Bryant said. "If you don't want it to, I can fix that for you."

"I announce myself because I cannot presume everyone checks the screen first."

"They don't?"

"Oddly, no. I can't understand it myself."

Bryant chuckled. "Okay, so hit me with today's hypothetical tech question, unrelated to any cases you're working."

Gabriel explained the situation.

"Nah," Bryant said. "It doesn't work like that. Spoofing numbers is easy enough, but it doesn't take much to prove they're spoofed. I know you don't like the technical details, so here's an example. If I used your phone number to send nude pics to my girlfriend, those pics would never appear on *your* phone. And if I started texting *your* girlfriend while spoofing *your* phone number, my texts would certainly never appear midstream in your conversation thread with her."

"Nor in her thread with me. Is that correct?"

"Right. She'd get an entirely new conversation thread, seemingly from your number. Now, having said all that, I'll add the usual caveat—there's a chance I'm full of shit. Tech is always advancing, especially black-market tech. Right now, though, I don't know of any way someone could do what you've described. If anyone can, then they have serious skills. Or the cash to rent them."

Gabriel signed off with the usual "I'll wire a donation to your college fund," along with the usual promise to pass on Bryant's hello to his grandmother. Then he hung up, thought a bit, and pulled out his laptop to begin searching.

There were many reasons for one spouse to want the other dead. In fact, no other relationship seemed to end in murder quite so often. Putting aside domestic violence, the top reasons to kill one's spouse were sex and money. More accurately, infidelity and inheritance.

He had Heather Nansen's phone records, along with a program designed by Bryant to analyze those—cross-referencing calls received and made, noting length and attempting to match the numbers to ones found online. Once analyzed, he had to dissect that data, looking for outliers and patterns.

Here he found both: outliers and patterns. Namely, multiple instances of ten- to fifteen-minute calls to numbers Heather only ever dialed once, all within a brief period, all the numbers tracing to the same type of business. Private investigators.

Six months ago, she'd been trying to hire an investigator. That was what the pattern suggested. Contact one, explain the situation, and ultimately, decide against hiring. She had something in mind, something she wanted investigated. All those calls came *before* the break-ins, suggesting no link there.

In the end, his digging circled back to the restaurant. Eclipse. To its financial health. It didn't take long for Gabriel to form his own diagnosis: the patient was on life support, and really, the smart thing to do would be to pull the plug. No incentive would have convinced him to invest in the restaurant. Despite its popularity, it leaked money like a sieve, which suggested someone was siphoning off profits.

He continued digging, through both public records and not-so-public ones. He was playing a hunch, and it didn't take long to confirm it.

When opening a business like a restaurant, one needs invest-ment capital. Those initial investors are the ones with the most to lose, arguably even more than Alan Nansen, who could ride his rep-utation to a new venture. The investors were also the ones directly affected by any misappropriation of funds.

There were a minor and a major investor in Eclipse. The minor one? Heather's parents. And the major? Heather herself, who had funded the venture almost singlehandedly.

Heather Nansen's degree was in business, which she used work-ing for both Eclipse and her mother's firm. That led to a second call, to Ricky, with questions about his own MBA, and the role he played in his father's business. The legal role, that is.

"Sure, I do handle the money," Ricky said when Gabriel asked about finances. "Dad began shifting that over to me when I started my degree. Now it's all mine. I control the piggy bank. Dad just signs your checks."

"Are you trained to find evidence of mismanagement? Questionable accounting?"

"An MBA is like a law degree. You can't be an expert in *all* law, and I'm not one in all aspects of running a business. But I happen to like number crunching—and Dad needs that more than he needs marketing and advertising—so I learned more about the financial side than other MBAs might. I don't do our accounting, but I oversee it. In a business like this, there's always someone looking to skim."

"If I send you some financial records for Nansen's business, can you tell me if anything looks suspicious?"

"Sure."

Twenty minutes later, Ricky called back with a yes. Or "Hell, yeah."

"Someone's raiding this piggy bank. Ricky said there's no way a restaurant that busy should see profit this low."

That suggested the person siphoning out money was Alan Nansen. Heather likely had the skills to spot discrepancies, and if she'd suspected someone other than her husband, she'd have been quick to inform on the culprit.

Gabriel could understand Nansen wanting a bigger share of the profit—he was the talent, the vision, and the one putting in the hours. But skimming would be more understandable if the investors were faceless corporate sponsors. When it was his wife's money? That was unacceptable.

Given the amount of the investment, Gabriel presumed that, like Olivia, Heather had received a trust fund. Wealthy parents wanting to make their only child's life easier at the time she needed it most—when she was young and establishing her own life, rather than waiting on an inheritance.

He suspected the lion's share of that trust had gone into Eclipse. What if Heather then discovered her husband was stealing from their nest egg, *her* birthright? And where was the money going? A mistress? Drugs? Gambling? Not back into their own bank accounts, that was sure.

Had she sought a private investigator to answer her questions… and then decided on another solution? One that would mean she didn't need to turn over half her remaining assets to Alan in a divorce court?

Certainly, private investigators were not supposed to share client information, but if Heather hadn't hired one, it was a gray area. Gabriel saw two on Heather's list that he knew would happily profit from exploiting that gray area and selling him details. He would discuss this with Olivia over dinner.

He checked his watch. It was past seven. He'd have thought she'd have called by now.

He reached for his phone, only to discover it wasn't beside his elbow. He looked about the kitchen table, where he'd set up a temporary office.

Oh, yes. He'd been so deep in thought earlier that he'd left his phone in his jacket. He retrieved that to find a text from Olivia, sent over an hour ago, asking whether he wanted to meet up and investigate together.

Before he could call back, he saw another message, more recent. *Johnson = cold-blooded SOB who deserves Hunt. Well, if I'm right. Found a few things. Incl what set him on Nansens. Going to talk to HN. Call me!*

Olivia was heading out to talk to Heather Nansen...apparently having decided that Johnson was responsible for Alan's death. Which meant she had no idea what Heather might be capable of.

Gabriel hit Olivia's number. When it rang through to voice mail, he grabbed his jacket and hurried out.

TWENTY-FOUR

OLIVIA

I MET Heather at her house. She quickly got over her surprise at me showing up on her doorstep and invited me in. I accepted a coffee this time. I hadn't heard back from Gabriel, and it looked like it was going to be a long night, possibly without dinner.

"One angle we'd like to pursue is uncovering the identity of the person attempting the break-ins," I said. "Presumably, the same person sent Alan those texts, and if we can prove it, we have our case."

She nodded. Said nothing, just nodded.

I went through my usual spiel on the search for alternative suspects...or at least one Gabriel could put forward to raise that Hail Mary of reasonable doubt.

Do you know of anyone who might have a grudge against you? Anyone at all?

We'd done this at our first meeting, and she seemed annoyed at me bringing it up again, but I said, "You've had time to think about it. Is there no one?"

She fluttered her hands. "Of course, there's always *someone*. If you've gotten through life without making enemies, count yourself very lucky."

"Oh, believe me, I haven't."

"I'm not the type who makes them naturally. Sure, there might be an ex who isn't thrilled with me, or a frenemy from my past, but no one who'd want revenge on this scale. I just don't have that sort of personality." She paused. "Alan does. *Did*, I mean. He could be…abrasive."

"All right, you can also hurt people accidentally. For example, in literal accidents. Like with a car."

She tensed.

"Have you or Alan ever been in an accident? One where you were at fault? Where someone was hurt? Possibly killed?"

I waited for the denials. She said nothing.

"This might jog your memory." I took out my phone and read the anonymous e-mail. "Dear Mr. Johnson, Two years ago, you lost your wife in an accident on North End Road. Another vehicle took the corner too fast. The driver lost control and hit your car, knocking it off the road. The driver then fled the scene without stopping to see whether you were all right. I know what happened because I was a passenger in that car. My husband was that driver. I begged him to call 911, but he refused and threatened me. If I'd had any idea how serious the accident was, I would have done something. I saw the news of your wife's death the next day, and I have never forgiven myself for my cowardice. No apology can ever bring her back, but I need you to know how sorry I am. I've anonymously wired you money. If you don't want it, please donate it appropriately."

I looked up from the screen. "Do you want to tell me again what happened to your second vehicle?"

"How—how did you get—?" she stammered.

"Does it matter? I know this is you. If you want to deny it, well, then we lose our best hope of finding the person whose harassment led to you getting a gun."

A long pause. Then she nodded. "Yes, that was me. But I did it anonymously—the e-mail, the money transfer. I don't see how Mr. Johnson could have known."

"Nothing is anonymous," I said. "Not if you're motivated enough to dig."

"So how do we prove he's the one who harassed me, who sent those texts to Alan?"

"Well, first, I'm going to need to borrow your phone."

TWENTY-FIVE

GABRIEL

GABRIEL COULD not get hold of Olivia. It wasn't the first time. In the past, though, most communication issues—at least, of the technical variety—had been fae in origin, purposely blocking them or sending messages from their accounts. The current communication problem, however, did not seem to be a fae issue so much as the very ordinary sort Gabriel and Olivia dealt with far too often—a breakdown of communication on a purely personal level.

When Olivia did finally get his message, she texted…which was not quite what he'd asked for.

What's up? she asked.

He sent back two words. *Call me.*

Can't. In the middle of something.

I need to speak to you, he replied.

Text?

That gave him pause. He couldn't very well text and say that he thought their client was actually guilty. That left a record. But saying nothing endangered Olivia.

Leave Heather, he sent, hoping that wasn't too cryptic.

Done. Now, gotta run. Talk soon.

What exactly did that mean? *Done?* That she'd spoken to Heather and moved on? Or was she—as Olivia herself would say—blowing him off?

Yep, totally ignoring Heather. Got it.

He flipped to another text, one that had come in a few minutes ago from Rose.

After you've spoken to Liv, come see me, please. No matter how late. I want to talk.

After you've spoken to Liv...

What did that mean?

Gabriel could pretend he didn't know, but there was only one scenario he might imagine, given that message.

Olivia knew about his nighttime visits to Seanna.

Which meant that Olivia was—again to use her vernacular—pissed. And when she was pissed, she didn't want anything to do with him. She was indeed blowing him off. Staying away until she'd finished pursuing a thread on the case, not wanting their personal issues to distract her from work.

Earlier, she'd been at the office, looking for him, wanting to confront him. And then, while waiting, she found some fresh lead, and she was off on that, putting him aside.

He could take comfort in the fact that she wasn't so furious that she'd sought him out immediately, work be damned. Except, if she was angry, he'd almost prefer that. Cold rage was worse. It boded worse.

She's finally had enough. She's done with you.

He stifled Gwynn's voice. Gwynn's *fears*, more accurately. Whatever consciousness remained of the fae king, he was Gabriel's guide, not his enemy. Gwynn's was the voice that said, "Seriously, you're keeping secrets from her again?" The fear came from Gabriel's own memories of Gwynn's mistakes with Matilda.

That realization hardly helped at this moment. What Gabriel *felt* was still that old fear.

She's had enough. She can't even be bothered telling you off.

He sent back one last text: *May I join you, in whatever you're doing?*

Mmm. Bad idea. Sorry. Love to have you along, but right now, that just gets complicated. Will call soon... I hope!

He looked at his phone. Beneath the Gwynn fears, he felt something else. An unease he knew well—a sixth sense that Olivia was in trouble.

Was she?

Or was that an excuse for what he wanted to do?

His finger hovered over an app that tracked her phone.

She said no. That he was not to join her.

But I'm worried.

She said—

Gabriel hit the button.

⤳

RICKY had installed tracking devices in all their phones after Gabriel and Olivia came far too close to dying of exposure after falling into a river. They hadn't agreed to use that app only in emergencies...because *that* went without saying. It was a matter of trust.

Was Gabriel breaking that trust now?

He honestly wasn't sure. That was the problem with living a life where trust had always been the one luxury he could not afford. While other people seemed to hopscotch easily through the landscape of relationships, he navigated it like a swamp, with quicksand and pythons and piranhas at every step.

He knew he should never use the app to keep tabs on her. That was obviously wrong. Nor would he ever use it to meet up with her, rather than texting to see whether she was free. It *was* only for emergencies, when he could not otherwise contact her and had reason for alarm.

Half of that applied now. Given what he'd learned about Heather, he had reason for alarm. Yet...well, he *could* contact her, couldn't he? But it wasn't in the way he needed to contact her—she was refusing to speak to him, and so he could not properly warn her. Did that make this an exception?

He believed he genuinely felt that sixth sense of concern, and yet he feared imagining it as an excuse to go to Olivia, to apologize and make things right. And if he *was* imagining it, then showing up and ignoring her explicit wishes would only upset her more.

He didn't know. When he tracked that signal and saw where she'd gone, though, he forgot the question entirely in a surge of exasperation and alarm.

Olivia was in a park. Not a playground safely within the city limits, but a picnic area five miles outside of it, one that would be closed past dark. It was already dusk.

The urge to text: *What the hell are you doing?* was nearly overwhelming. He might have, too, if he didn't know *exactly* what she was doing.

Meeting someone.

For the case, that is. The thought of Olivia meeting a lover for a tryst entered his head only as the fleeting notion that, for ordinary people, that was exactly why they'd go to a park past dark. Not Olivia. For her, this out-of-the-way spot suggested a covert encounter of the professional sort.

She must be meeting Heather Nansen there. The Nansens lived at that end of the city, and Olivia needed to discuss something in absolute privacy—completely ignoring his warnings. Yes, this *was* an excellent spot for a private meeting…and it was also an excellent spot to be murdered by a killer and have your body dragged into the nearby woods.

Gabriel pulled his car into an overgrown lane near the park. The Jag rolled down the rutted path, each jolt giving him one more thing to grumble about, along with the knowledge that if he did damage the vehicle, at least he could guarantee Olivia would regret *one* part of this escapade.

He also acknowledged the unfairness of his word choice. An escapade suggested Olivia routinely traipsed into danger unaware, needing rescue. Untrue. Or, at least, two-thirds of it was untrue. She was never unaware of the danger, and she didn't require rescue any more than he did. He would prefer to think he strode into danger, though. *Traipsing* was really more Olivia's style.

He walked through the forest to the park, hearing every slosh of his loafers on the muddy ground, feeling cold water seep in. With the full moon, he could see the picnic benches and pavilions but no sign of Olivia.

He cursed Ricky for not finding an app that more accurately pinpointed location. Again, unjust. The issue was the inadequacy of GPS in general. He knew Olivia was within a few hundred feet. Perhaps hiding in the shadows of the pavilion, awaiting Heather?

He took out his phone. The screen shone far too brightly, so he shielded it and then reread the text stream.

He should tell Olivia he was here. Admit wrongdoing and let her know he was nearby. *Yes, I know you said to stay away, but I was concerned, and so I am here.*

His fingers hovered over the keypad. Then a twig cracked in the park. Gabriel stepped forward…and his loafer stayed behind, stuck in the mud.

With a grunt of annoyance, he balanced on one foot, backing up to slide his foot into—

"Don't move."

Gabriel turned. That was the problem with a voice from nowhere, telling you not to move—reacting to the surprise, one naturally moves. A man lunged at him, a blade flashing. Gabriel backed up fast, his hands out.

"I'm unarmed," he said.

The man waved the knife, which would have been far more threatening if he'd looked as if he had the faintest clue how to use it. No, strike that. In Gabriel's experience, those who didn't know how to use a weapon posed an even greater danger—that of harming someone unintentionally. What mattered was that the blade appeared clean, as did the man's clothing, meaning he had not used that knife on Olivia.

"I'm unarmed," Gabriel repeated. "However, I am not alone, Mr. Johnson."

The man tensed, confirming Gabriel was correct in his guess. Johnson inched forward, knife raised.

"I know who you are, too, Gabriel Walsh," he said. "A lawyer. A defense lawyer."

He spit the words the way one might say "serial killer." No, having defended serial killers, Gabriel knew people voiced *that* term with far less venom.

"You're her lawyer," Johnson continued. "That murderess, Heather Nansen."

"The term is 'murderer,' and has been since the time of Lizzie Borden, but in this case, I believe you are also missing the adjective 'alleged.'"

"Lawyers." Johnson sneered. "So it *was* you, wasn't it? You sent that text from her phone."

"Ah."

"Ah?"

It was apparently the wrong response. Johnson lunged, and Gabriel attempted to dodge, but he was really too big for dodging, and the knife caught his sleeve, slicing through a very expensive jacket and shirt. Skin, too, given the stab of pain, but his *arm* would mend. Gabriel swung up, attempting to disarm Johnson, and—to his chagrin—failing.

So Gabriel charged, barreling into Johnson, who evidently did not expect to be attacked by an unarmed man. Johnson let out a yelp. He also swung the knife, the tip of it scraping Gabriel's jaw.

Gabriel punched Johnson. The smaller man flew backward but kept his balance, raising the knife as he ran at Gabriel.

"And that's enough of that," a voice said.

TWENTY-SIX

GABRIEL

GABRIEL DODGED the charge and swung around to see Olivia holding her gun on Johnson.

"It's like rock, paper, scissors," she said. "Except in a game of fist, knife, gun, the gun always wins. Stop right there, Keith."

Johnson peered at her. "You...you're..."

"The dumb chick who wanted to trade in a Shelby Cobra for an Audi? Well, duh. No one's *that* stupid."

Johnson snarled and lunged at Gabriel.

Olivia fired a warning shot over Johnson's shoulder. "Did I say *enough?* You've already ruined one of his jackets." She glanced at Gabriel. "Which is the price he pays for ignoring my instructions."

"I know you're upset about what Rose said, and you don't want to have anything to do with me right now, but I sensed you were in danger."

Her brows shot up. "You thought I was refusing backup because I'm pissy?"

"Not...exactly."

She shook her head. "I said no for exactly this reason." She waved at the two of them. "Because I had things under control, and bringing you in seemed more likely to end up exactly the way it did, you barging onto my stage after I so carefully set—"

Johnson spun, slashing the knife at Gabriel, who dodged while Olivia leapt forward, gun pointed at Johnson's head.

"Yeah, sorry," she said. "Just because we're bickering doesn't mean we aren't paying attention."

"I wouldn't call it bick—" Gabriel began, but she stopped him with a look.

"Can you move behind him, please, Gabriel?" she asked. "In case he decides to bolt."

"I have no idea what's—" Johnson said.

"You killed your wife."

Gabriel's head shot up. Fortunately, he was on the other side of Johnson now, so the man didn't see his surprise.

"What?" Johnson said. "My wife was *murdered* by Alan Nansen because he lost control and hit my car and *left* the scene."

"Mmm, he bears responsibility, sure. His actions could have killed her. But yours did. You took advantage of the scenario he set up. Kathy was seriously injured, and you…well, you just waited to see what would happen. How badly injured was she? What if you were a little slow to call 911? What if you just…observed for a while? I've been called cold-blooded, but I can't imagine doing that to anyone, let alone someone I loved."

"You have no idea what—" Johnson cut himself short. "I didn't do that."

"You did, and you got away with it because they never caught the other driver, so there was no reason to dig deeper, no reason to suspect your story. But then Heather Nansen had an inconvenient

attack of conscience and sent you an apology and blood money. You tracked her down and decided to kill two birds with one bullet. Put Heather in such fear for her life that she got a gun. Then you sent Alan a text message—"

"What?"

Olivia paused, her eyes narrowing. After a moment, she went on. "You lured Alan home. Heather shot him. But the police didn't find the texts, so it was ruled an accident, which wasn't what you wanted. You contacted the police with a tip that Alan had been lured home by his wife."

"No, I never..." He trailed off. "I never did *any* of that."

"Which isn't what you were going to say." Olivia gave him that same piercing look. "You objected to the texts and the call. Those two things specifically."

Gabriel caught her eye and motioned.

She gave a long, slow nod. Then she said, "You broke in and stole Heather's phone to—"

"I never stole—I never did anything. You're crazy." He stepped back. "I'm leaving now, and if you try to stop me..."

He backed into Gabriel and then wheeled, brandishing the knife.

"Put the knife down, Keith," she said. "We're just talking. Warning you. We have proof that you were the person who broke into the Nansens' house, who came back twice more. Clearly, you were trying to spook her into buying—"

"I was only trying to spook them, okay? You know what they did to my wife. Not me. Them. That was my revenge. Scaring them."

"For murdering your beloved wife? Seems a little...underwhelming, don't you think?"

He glared at Olivia. "I hadn't decided what to do."

"Oh, I think you had. I think you'd decided to kill Heather Nansen to safeguard your secret. You're just a really, really shitty assassin. Three times you tried to get into the house. You only managed it once, but you kept coming back, hoping to silence her before another attack of conscience sent her to the police. Heather buying the gun and shooting her husband? That was a completely unexpected outcome."

"You have no idea what you're talking—"

"Keith Johnson," Olivia said. "You are guilty of the murder of Kathy Johnson." She lifted the gun. "Now run."

The color drained from Johnson's face. He took a slow step back. "No..."

A snarl rippled from the forest, and the alpha hound shot out. Johnson spun. Then Lloergan burst from the trees on his left side. She was herding him, not stopping him, but when Johnson saw her—a smaller cŵn, a disfigured cŵn—he let out a howl of rage and charged. Lloergan stopped short, confused. Johnson kept charging, the knife raised.

"No!" Olivia shouted and ran at them.

Gabriel tackled Johnson. They grappled, and again, that knife sliced far too close to his face. He let Johnson swing it wildly and then grabbed his arm, pinning it before wrenching the knife away.

Gabriel tossed the knife aside and picked up Johnson by the shirtfront, lifting him until he was on his tiptoes.

"Would you like mercy?" Gabriel asked.

Johnson blinked hard. Then, "Y-yes. Yes, please."

"Tell the truth." He held the man out to Olivia. "To her."

Johnson swallowed. When he said nothing, Gabriel whistled, and Lloergan's ears perked up. The alpha hound started forward, his head lowered. More cŵns slid from the dark forest.

"It—it happened so fast," Johnson blurted. "The accident. With Kathy. And then...I don't know what came over me. I passed in and out of consciousness, and I was confused—"

Gabriel shook him. "The *truth*."

Another pause. The hounds inched closer.

"S-she wanted a divorce. We'd been fighting, and I was angry. Okay? The accident happened, and I just—I snapped. I didn't think. I wanted a way out, and I saw it, so I... I waited. I just waited. I didn't *do* anything to her."

"And then Heather Nansen contacted you..."

"*They* started this. They hit our car. It was their fault, and that bitch was going to tell the police. I knew she was. I'd suffered enough—all those nights worrying that someone would find out about Kathy. I didn't *do* anything to her, and now I might go to *jail* for it? That wasn't fair, not when it was their fault. But I never touched that bitch. I broke in the first time and got spooked. I tried a couple more times, but she kept hearing me, so I gave up. I didn't steal anything from her. I didn't text anyone or call the police about anything."

Gabriel looked at Olivia. "Is that enough?"

"I already had enough," she said.

He lifted one shoulder in a half-shrug. She might have had enough to be reasonably certain. Now that certainty was absolute, and he could see the relief on her face.

"Enough for mercy?" Johnson croaked.

Olivia stepped forward. "Your wife had a punctured lung. You watched her die. You *listened* to her die. At first, you weren't sure how badly she was injured, but eventually, she'd have begun wheezing. Slowly suffocating. Gasping for breath. And you watched and waited. I will give you the exactly the amount of mercy you gave her."

She took another step forward. "Run, Mr. Johnson. Run as fast as you can. And when you can't run anymore—when your lungs give out, and you lie there gasping for air, remember your wife."

Gabriel threw Johnson aside. The man stumbled to his feet. Then the alpha cŵn leapt at him, snarling, and Johnson looked up to see the pack of red-eyed giant black hounds, ringing him, leaving only a gap into the forest.

He bolted for that gap, and the hounds pursued.

TWENTY-SEVEN

OLIVIA

SO THE Cŵn Annwn were not infallible after all.

After Johnson died in the Hunt, Ioan and I convened with Ricky and Gabriel, and we figured out what had happened. First, I got the "discovery" story—how the Cŵn Annwn found Johnson. One of the Huntsmen had an Audi, which he'd taken in for its annual servicing. There, he'd bumped into Johnson and gotten the twinge that put a target on Johnson's head.

Ioan had picked up the vehicle for the Huntsman, and he'd sought out Johnson in a casual conversation. When he looked into his eyes, he got a memory flash of the newspaper headline, along with a surge of guilt that confirmed he was a Cŵn Annwn target. So Ioan concluded Nansen must have had fae blood and Johnson killed him. An incorrect deduction. Yes, Johnson had felt some responsibility for Nansen's death, thinking that his attempts to break in had caused Heather to shoot her husband. But the death that warranted Cŵn Annwn justice was actually that of Kathy Johnson, who must have had fae blood.

A crossed wire, which caused Ioan to accuse Johnson of the wrong murder. But when it came to what counted, he'd been absolutely correct. Johnson was a killer who deserved Cŵn Annwn justice.

As for Heather Nansen, Gabriel's independent investigation suggested there was a very good reason Johnson had denied stealing her phone, sending those texts and contacting the police. He hadn't. The simple explanation was, it seemed, correct—that no one had framed Heather for murder. She'd taken advantage of the break-in attempts to obtain a gun, and then she'd lured her husband home.

Gabriel wasn't going to drop her case. We now believed she was guilty, but proving it was up to the prosecution. And I was fine with that. This was not my case to judge.

My case had been Keith Johnson, and I had my answer there.

GABRIEL and I spent the drive to Cainsville talking about Heather's case, which meant we didn't need to discuss our own issue. Not until we got home, and the door closed behind us.

"I'm sorry I didn't tell you about Seanna," he said. "I thought I could handle it by myself."

"The point of being with someone, Gabriel, is that you don't have to handle things alone."

"I just wanted…"

"To fix it without upsetting me. I know. But what do you think would upset me more? Navigating this problem together from the first time Seanna pulled that crap? Or watching you struggle for months and not knowing what was going on?"

He nodded.

I continued, "You're right that this makes me wonder whether we made the right choices with Seanna. Choices I championed. But that only means that I take responsibility for resolving this with Rose."

He paused in the front hall. "I'll understand if you'd rather I just dropped you off and went back to Chicago."

I sighed and shook my head, and then waved him into the living room. "This is what we need to work on, Gabriel. Being upset with you doesn't mean I want to get away from you. Okay, maybe, if I'm pissed enough, I'll need time to myself. Temporarily. But I'm not..." I turned to face him. "I'm not going anywhere."

His nod claimed he understood, but the wary look in his eyes said he wasn't so sure. Or that my declaration wasn't enough. Wasn't clear enough. Did I mean I wasn't going anywhere today? In the near future?

I motioned for him to sit on the sofa. Then I took the other end, my purse still in my hand. He kept looking at it, as if that belied my assurance that I wasn't about to flee.

"When I was a teenager," I said, "sometimes guys gave rings to girls they'd been dating for a while. Not an engagement ring—they were too young for that. But a ring that said marriage was where they were heading, eventually. A promise ring."

"Would you like...?" he began cautiously.

I burst into a laugh. "Uh, no. That isn't a hint. Not exactly how I operate, if you haven't figured that out."

I reached into my purse and took out a rolled-up sheet of paper. When I handed it to him, he hesitated.

"I'm not serving you a summons," I said.

He took the paper and then saw the ring on it.

"Yeah, it's a ring," I said. "But just ignore that."

His brows arched.

I made a face. "I mean you don't have to wear it. I know you don't wear jewelry. It's symbolic."

He tugged the ring off and turned it over in his hand.

"Be happy it isn't one of those high school promise rings with a diamond chip," I said. "Or a big rock of cubic zirconia."

He held the ring up. It wasn't exactly the result of days of careful shopping—I'd been in a hurry—but I'd tried to choose with care, visiting several stores before I found a simple band with a pale blue sapphire.

"Yes, it matches your eyes," I said.

He smiled and slipped on the ring.

"It probably won't—"

"It fits." He looked at me. "Thank you."

"Well, like I said, that's not really the gift. The ring is symbolic. And even the gift isn't actually..." I exhaled. "Just open the paper."

He unscrolled it to find a picture.

"This is..." He tilted his head as he studied the photo. "It's the cabin I rented for us last winter. The one on the lake. Yes?"

"I offered to buy it."

He glanced up. "It's for sale?"

"Not exactly. I made the owner a good offer, and he accepted."

He frowned. "I hope you didn't pay more than necessary."

I laughed. "Not exactly the point here, Gabriel, but don't worry—my offer was decent but fair. I made sure of that. Particularly because I expect you to pay half."

His brows rose.

"Yep, like I said, it's not really a gift. But you have your condo, and I have my house here, so what we need is a place that's *ours*. A vacation home. Because, of course, we require a third residence."

His lips twitched in a smile. "We do."

"I can certainly pay the full—"

"No." He set the photo aside. "This is what I would prefer. Joint ownership."

"Good. We'll consider it an investment if that makes us feel less indulgent. But the point, between the ring and the joint property, is that I'm not going anywhere. I'd love to say that's a guarantee, but nothing is. We just solved two cases of spousal homicide, so clearly, even marriage isn't a promise of happily ever after. Which isn't to say that I'm against that, at some point, but if we did get married now, my concern is that we'd be doing it to lock this in, rather than because we're ready."

"I don't want that." He paused. "I mean jumping to marriage. Marriage itself is fine, but you're right—at this point, I would want it as a guarantee. Which it isn't." He lifted the paper. "This says the same thing. That we're committed to making it work long term."

"Yes." I looked at him. "Is that what you want?"

He held my gaze. "It is definitely what I want."

"Good," I said.

As I leaned over to kiss him, something crumpled in his pocket and the smell of baked goods wafted out.

"Is that...?" I began.

He cleared his throat. "It's the anniversary of the day we met, so I, uh, got you..."

When he trailed off, I pulled the bag from his pocket and laughed. "It's a scone."

"Yes. Which, when compared to your gifts, seems..." Another throat clearing. "I will do better next time."

I threw my arms around his neck. "The fact that you remember the day we met is all the anniversary gift I need. Especially when..." I lifted up his ear. "I totally forgot." I took a bite of the scone, tossed the bag aside. "But if you want to give me a better gift, I have a few ideas in mind. Ones you can deliver right now. If you feel compelled to make amends."

He chuckled. "I do," he said, and lowered me onto the sofa.